DARK
HOUSES

A gripping detective thriller full of suspense

HELEN H. DURRANT

Published 2016 by Joffe Books, London.

www.joffebooks.com

© Helen Durrant

ISBN-13: 978-1-911021-48-3

Prologue

Murder.

It was a skill. It was addictive. It was his life.

The skill lay in the planning; making sure you wouldn't get caught. The addiction was incurable. There was no rehab for people like him.

He watched the young man go into the café. He already knew his name — Neville Dakin. They had never spoken, but he was about to change that. He'd lined up Neville Dakin weeks ago. On one occasion their eyes had met, just fleetingly. There had been a spark in that look. And then he knew.

Soon he would strike again — three times. And it would be Neville who took the blame. The police would see only what he put in front of them. It would never occur to them that Neville had been set up. Then, just as he had in the past, he'd walk clean away.

He sat down in a chair facing the young man. "I don't talk to strangers," Neville said.

"But I'm not a stranger. You know me. Look closer."

The young man peered at him. "Are you sure?"

The café was empty. There were no prying eyes. He couldn't pass up this opportunity. "Yes, I'm your friend. You must remember me." The smile he gave Neville was open and confident.

Neville shook his head. "Sorry. I forget things, you see. It's the pills. They make me weird. They make me sleep as well. Sometimes I wake up in the morning and I don't even know who I am."

"In that case they aren't doing you any good. You should stop taking them."

"I have to take them. I've been ill."

"But you're better now? You look fine."

"It's not what I look like. It's what's going on up here that matters." Neville tapped the side of his head.

"I can help you recover."

"I'll never be right. They said so."

"They get it wrong."

"Are you real?" Neville leaned forward, reaching out to touch him, and he ducked away. "You're not, are you?" Neville said. "But I don't mind."

Neville smiled shyly.

"I don't think much of where they've put you." He stirred his coffee. "That block's where they put all the no-hopers they want to hide away. Everyone will think you're a nutter. You should complain."

"I am a nutter. That's the whole point. That's what's wrong with me. But I like it there. I have my own room," said Neville.

"You won't be happy on your own."

"That's what Edna said. Will you visit me?"

"No — but you can visit me. You can help me with something if you like."

"Will you take me out?" Neville said.

"Do you like girls, Neville?" Girls. Just the hook he needed.

"I don't know any."

"When you come out with me you'll meet some. If you do as I say, the girls will like you — a lot."

"They don't usually like me. I think I frighten them."

"Not this time."

"Can I kiss them?"

"Yes, and lots more beside. We'll have some fun."

Neville blushed. "I've never been with a girl."

"Do as I tell you, and I'll give you one of your very own."

"Can I tell Edna?"

"No. This is our secret. You can keep a secret, can't you?"

Neville nodded enthusiastically. "When do we start?"

"What medication are you on?"

Neville took a bottle of pills from his pocket and showed him.

"Those aren't good for you." He snatched them away and poured them out into his pocket. "These are better." He opened a packet and emptied them into Neville's bottle. "Take these instead. I promise — you'll see a difference right away."

Chapter 1

He heard the *tap, tap* of her high heels on the cobbles of the dimly lit street. She was getting close. He turned the light out. The flicker from the open fire would be more inviting. He stuck the poker deep into the glowing coals. He wanted it good and hot. Good and hot. The thought sent a shiver of need running through his body.

Silence. Her shoes had stopped tapping. Horrified that she might have changed direction, he peeked through a hole in the threadbare curtains. All was well. She was standing a few yards from the house, balancing on one foot. She was fiddling with the strap on one of those stupid high-heeled shoes.

It was time to make his move.

He stood in the doorway, whistling. She was close enough now that he could smell her cheap perfume. She wore an ultra-short skirt wrapped like cling-film around her thighs, a low-cut top and a pink fake fur jacket. A cheap tart. He'd chosen well.

"Oatmeal or mocha?" he asked. He held out two samples of paint. "I have to get it right or the wife will kill me. It's our first place," he said. "Not much, I know — a small terrace on a back street in Oldston, but it's all ours."

"What's it going with?"

She was chewing gum and, despite her youth, she had a couple of teeth missing.

"Flowery wallpaper. The wife chose it for the chimney breast. It's a vivid orange with cream. I don't have much of an eye for this sort of thing."

"Let's take a look," she said with a friendly smile.

His spine tingled. This was so easy. She pushed past him through the front door. He followed her in, grinning and stroking himself.

* * *

Day One

"It's not pretty," the pathologist Natasha Barrington warned.

Detective Inspector Stephen Greco walked into the room. He had seen a lot of horrific sights in his time, but this was one of the worst.

"Grim, isn't it?" That was a major understatement. "I'll let the CSI do their stuff, then they can get her down," she said.

The young woman hung from an oak beam set in the low ceiling. She was naked. A rope bound one wrist to the beam. It wound around her neck several times, then tied the other wrist. Her arms were stretched horizontally and her head lolled forward onto her chest. Each ankle was tethered to chairs placed either side of her, splaying her legs apart. Her dark hair hung limp, blood-soaked, to her shoulders. Her eyes bulged and her tongue protruded.

Staring into hell.

"Who found her?"

"The owner, one Rashid Rahman. As you'll see from the sign outside, the house is for sale. It's unoccupied. A neighbour heard a noise, saw smoke coming from the chimney and rang him. He's in rather a state. He's gone next door for a shot of something strong. There's no sign of a break-in. The lock's intact, no broken windows. A PC looked all round and reckoned they must have had a key."

"Sergeant!" Greco called out, tapping on the window. "Get in here."

Sergeant Jed Quickenden, known as Speedy, had taken one look and dashed outside to throw up.

"Is he usually this squeamish?" Natasha asked Greco.

"Yes, I'm afraid he is."

"Even though it's my job, sights like this don't do me any good either. But we have to get on with it. We have our work to do . . . Anyway, the wound to her chest is what killed her. They cut into the chest wall with something sharp." She nodded at a poker lying on the floor beside her. "That, I suspect, was heated and used to burn a hole through her heart. There has been extensive burning to her face too." She winced as she looked at the girl's body. "The burning has made those holes in her cheeks. There has been a fire in the hearth. The embers are still warm."

"Anything else from your preliminary examination?"

"She was raped, and brutally too. I'll know more when I get her on the table. Not content with the burning, she's also been cut about the mouth and scalp. Her mouth has been cut crosswise extending up into the cheek like a cartoon of a wide smile."

"When, do you reckon?"

"Sometime last night. Late on, I'd say."

A woman spoke from behind them. "The clothing is interesting."

"This is Doctor Roxy Atkins, our new lead forensic expert," Natasha said. She introduced her to Greco and Quickenden, who was cowering in the background.

She was hidden in her coverall. All you could see was that she was small and slim. A wisp of black hair stuck out from under her hood.

"How so?" Greco asked.

"They appear to have been cut neatly from the body, I'd say with scissors. They've been folded and left on that chair over there. Her bag still has her purse and mobile in it. Her purse contains a debit card, a photo of her and a young man, and some cash. I'll bag everything up and look at it in the lab."

"Does the debit card have a name on it?" Greco asked.

"Jessie Weston," Roxy replied. "There's an envelope too. Her address is on the Link Road estate. You'll need to inform the next of kin, have her identified formally."

Quickenden took the envelope, now in an evidence bag, from Roxy and copied down the address.

"When will you do the post-mortem?" Greco asked.

"Later this morning," Natasha replied, checking her watch. "Say about eleven?"

"I think this is one we should attend," he told Quickenden, who muttered a reply.

"Okay, eleven it is then," Natasha said.

"Have the photos been taken?"

"Being done now," Roxy said.

"Don't keep her up there for a second longer than necessary," said Greco.

Natasha called to a man in a coverall who was taking photographs. "How long now, Mark?"

"Nearly there," he said.

This had not been done on the spur of the moment, in jealousy or rage. The trussing up, the torture, were horrifying. This was the work of a psychopath.

"I want you to find the next of kin. Take them to the Duggan and get a formal identification. Don't say anything other than that she's been killed. No details. Do you understand?" Greco said.

Quickenden nodded.

"I'll do what I can to make her more presentable," said Natasha.

"And don't go disappearing," Greco said to Quickenden.

The sergeant nodded. He wiped his face with a hankie.

Quickenden had tried to up his game since Greco became his DI. At least he'd managed to moderate his behaviour — and improve his appearance. His clothes were clean and ironed. He'd had his hair cut. But even Greco had to admit the new look did nothing for him. Quickenden just never looked right. He was tall and very thin. Short hair accentuated his long, thin face.

"Unless Green says otherwise, I want you on this one. No excuses. Have you got that?"

Quickenden nodded. Then he dashed outside and threw up again.

* * *

Greco knew he should go straight to the station and begin formulating a plan for the investigation. But first he had to shower and change. There was no way he could get though the day wearing the clothes he'd entered that room in. His OCD wouldn't let him. It had flared up again, brought on by the horror of what he'd just seen.

He'd go to his flat. That way, his ex-wife Suzy would never know. Together they had developed a strategy to keep his condition under control, and it had been working — until now. He didn't want her upset by this sudden setback.

He and Suzy were together again, but taking things slowly. It was she who wanted to try again after their divorce, and Greco was happy to agree. The divorce had made him miserable. It had been hard only seeing his daughter on designated weekends, and not being able to talk to Suzy properly. He was delighted when she'd admitted the divorce had been a mistake.

He'd kept his flat on because it was useful. When he was working late or had one of his bouts of insomnia it was simpler just to stay there. But it was an indulgence they couldn't afford for much longer. He really should consider putting it on the market

Suzy was helping him with his condition. She knew him better than anyone and recognised all the signs — the obsessive hand-washing, the preoccupation with hygiene, having everything exactly in its place. With her help he was confident he'd get on top of it. But not today. Today was an exception he couldn't tell her about.

Greco tore off his clothes and jumped into the shower as soon as he arrived. A new bar of soap and a torrent of hot water would hopefully wash away any contamination from that room. Not that Greco really believed there was any. He had that much rationality. After a thorough scrub and a mug of coffee he began to feel normal again. He'd needed this time out. If he was to function at his best, his head had to be clear, and free of obsessive-compulsive thoughts.

He put on fresh clothes, deciding to wear a lighter suit. The weather was getting warmer. It was late spring, and at last he could put away the overcoat he'd practically lived in all winter. A quick check in the mirror, a reminder to himself to get his hair cut, a tweak of his tie . . . he was ready to go.

He heard a key turn in the lock on the front door. It was Doris Hope, his cleaning lady. Apart from Suzy, Doris was the only other person to have a key. She came in three times a week, whether he'd been there or not, so the place was always spick and span.

"Hello, Mr Greco!" she said. "I'm glad I've caught you. No need to leave a note now, and anyway, it's better said in person."

"What is it, Mrs Hope?"

"I'm leaving you, I'm afraid." She threw her coat onto a chair and Greco tensed. "My Albert has retired now, you see. We've decided to go for one of those houses on Pierce Street, the old terraced cottages. It's a buy-to-let project.

It'll keep Albert out of trouble and bring in extra income to eke out our pensions."

"You're going to help him?" Greco picked up the coat and hung it up in the hallway.

"Not really. I'll be the gofer. It'll be me down the do-it-yourself shops buying stuff, making his sandwiches, keeping the place tidy, that sort of thing."

"I wish you luck. It's hard work I believe, but a popular undertaking these days. Always providing folk have the money."

"We've saved for most of our lives. But it's no good stashing money in the bank the way things are, is it?"

"So when do you want to go?"

"Today, after I've finished, if that's alright with you. I'll stick the key through the letterbox when I've locked up."

Greco nodded. "I'll pop round later with your wages. Thanks for all the time you've put in." He smiled at her.

"You're a treat to work for. You've been no trouble at all," she said, making her way into the kitchen. "I wish all my people had been like you."

Greco walked out to his car. Perhaps he should take Mrs Hope's leaving as a sign. Use it as the excuse he was looking for to ditch the flat once and for all and move in properly with Suzy. He'd give it some thought and talk it over with her later. In the meantime he had the case to think about.

The body of that poor girl was one of the most awful sights he'd ever witnessed. The killer had taken his time, inflicted intense pain and made her suffer until the very end. Was it personal? Did he have a private vendetta? Or, more terrifying, was it the beginning of a new nightmare for the town of Oldston? If this was the case, would his team even be allowed to get involved? Greco knew that moves were afoot to set up a 'Major Incident Team' to cover all serious crime committed in the Oldston, Leesworth and nearby Daneside areas. This team would be made up of CID officers handpicked from within the local stations along with others recruited from outside.

Greco didn't know any of the officers at Daneside, but he did know the people at Leesworth. DC Rockliffe had been offered a place on the new MIT but had already refused. DI Calladine would more than likely be considered too old. As for his own people — DC Grace Harper perhaps? She was good, and had showed promise during the last case they'd worked on. He couldn't see Quickenden being offered a place. He was too work-shy. Then there was him of course. But was that the way he wanted to go? And if he did, who would head up the MIT? He pulled into the car park at the Duggan Centre. His phone rang. It was DCI Colin Green from the station. This would be it — the final word on whether he was in or out of the case.

"Stephen," began Green. "I've seen the preliminary report. It's a bad one. Whoever did this needs catching fast, but we've got a problem. The new team we discussed is still a work in progress. This happened on our patch, so I'm afraid Oldston station has drawn the short straw. And that means you."

So there it was. His team was on its own once again.

"I did wonder whether or not the new squad would get it."

"We're no nearer than we were three months ago, when it was first mooted. Too few officers of the right calibre, and even fewer resources. However, there is help if you need it. Daneside have offered someone. Leesworth are already an officer down, so no joy there, but you must make full use of uniform. Get them to do the legwork. We have some good people, Stephen."

Trouble was, Greco could count those good people on the fingers of one hand. "Who's on the cards from Daneside?"

"A Sergeant Seddon. Good record, looking for promotion, sounds promising. I'll sort it."

"We should wait until we know what we're up against."

"Don't be coy about accepting the help, Stephen. We need this sorting quickly. We've already got the press outside the station, and they're baying for blood."

"They were quick off the mark. It's only been a few hours."

"Someone on that street rang them. Which means they'll have already sold what they know for a fat fee, and have no doubt been promised more if they keep their eyes peeled," Green said bitterly. "Since you will be going back there to interview the neighbours, be careful what is said. I don't mean you particularly, but the other members of your team."

"I understand, sir," Greco replied. "If this Sergeant Seddon is keen to join us, that's fine with me. I'm at the Duggan now. Quickenden and I will observe the PM then get back to the station."

But Quickenden was nowhere to be seen and his vehicle wasn't in the car park. He should be inside with the relatives, helping them through the identification of the body. So what had happened?

Chapter 2

Jed Quickenden took one look at the address and groaned.
Why did it have to be here? Why him? The spring sunshine
did nothing to make the Link Road estate look better. It
was a depressing, downtrodden place that the council, and
even the law, chose to ignore as much as possible.

But it was more than that for Quickenden. Ever since
Grady Gibbs's death he'd been avoiding the area. People
blamed him. Of course they knew Quickenden hadn't
wielded the knife himself, and most folk hadn't liked
Gibbs much either. But Gibbs had been one of their own,
and Quickenden was now very much on the other side.

He parked his car on a stretch of open ground and
stared up at the tower block. Jessie Weston had lived on
the twelfth floor with her mother Mavis and a younger
brother. He knew the lift only went as far as the sixth. "I'll
go up and get her," he told the uniformed officer who'd
accompanied him.

He hauled his lanky frame step by step up the last six
flights, gasping. He was seriously out of condition. Too
many fags, too much booze and precious little in the way
of exercise took its toll no matter how young you were. If
he wanted to keep this job he'd have to try harder. But was

he up to it? Greco had marked his card and was watching him like a hawk. It had got so bad Quickenden was rapidly getting sick of the whole police thing. If he could find some other way of earning a living, he'd get out.

Panting, the DS banged on the front door of flat 1207. No answer. He tried peering through the window but it was caked with dirt.

"Get lost!" a male voice shouted from inside.

"Police!" Quickenden bawled back. He was in no mood for a protracted argument.

"We ain't done nowt, so sling yer hook!" An empty beer can struck the inside of the window.

"It's about Jessie!" Quickenden shouted back. "I need to see her mother."

"What's the stupid cow done now?" Finally a dishevelled youth came to the door.

"Is Mavis Weston in?"

"No, she ain't come home in a while. I ain't got a clue where she's gone."

Now Quickenden had a problem. He needed a close relative to identify Jessie. Would this one do? "Can't you ring her? It is important."

"She don't answer."

"Who are you?"

"Jonathan Weston, Jessie's brother."

"How old are you, son?"

The young man was tall, slight and scruffily dressed. He looked about sixteen.

"Nineteen. Why? What d'you think I've done?"

"Nothing, Jonathan. This is about Jessie. Look, there's no easy way to say this . . ." Quickenden could tell the lad was losing interest. He kept looking back towards the TV and the football match he'd been watching. "I'm afraid Jessie's dead. She's been killed."

Someone scored a goal. The lad grunted. "You're kidding me. You don't expect me to believe that."

"It's the truth."

"What happened?"

He didn't seem much surprised.

"It's a murder enquiry, so I can't say much."

"Murder? Our Jessie? Got that one wrong, mate. Jessie will be working about now, down at the Crown."

"No, Jonathan, she isn't. In fact, that's why I'm here . . . I want you to come with me and identify her body."

"Why bother? You seem to know who you've got."

"It has to be done formally by a relative, someone who knew her well. Why not get your coat and come with me. I've got a car down there and an officer will bring you right back."

"You're not having me on, are you?"

"No. I wish I was. Your sister has been killed. It's no joke, and we are searching for her murderer."

Jonathan Weston grabbed a coat off a hook behind the door and stepped out onto the deck. He looked at Quickenden. "Won't throw up, will I? Never seen a dead body before."

* * *

The post-mortem room had never held any fears for Greco. He liked the clinical cleanliness of the gleaming stainless steel and the white floors. They were somehow comforting. He stood on a raised platform only five feet from where Natasha Barrington would perform her art.

Jessie Weston's body was laid out on a table, covered in a white sheet. He shuddered. She was so young, too young to have had her life so brutally snatched from her. A long list of questions swirled in Greco's mind and he tried to order them. First, he had to determine the motive.

Natasha Barrington smiled and waved at him as she and her assistants entered the room.

"Alone, I see," she said. "Your sergeant got cold feet again?"

Greco didn't reply. Quickenden had gained a reputation. He had been warned about his conduct during the last big case they'd worked on. Greco didn't want to be on his back again.

"She'd been dead about ten hours when she was found. So I'd put time of death at one this morning." Natasha removed the sheet and reached for a microphone.

Greco wondered where had she been until that time on a week night.

"We have the body of a female, one Jessie Weston. Her brother gave her age as twenty-six. She's of slim build and otherwise healthy." She leaned over to examine the body more closely. "There are a number of injuries on the upper torso and the face." She stood to one side, making way for the photographer. "Most of these are burns. To the face, chest and arms. The right nipple has been completely burned away."

Greco felt sick.

"There are what appear to be knife cuts to the body, on both thighs and the belly. She has several much deeper lacerations to the face and scalp. The scalp wounds will have bled profusely. They are deep and long."

She parted Jessie's hair carefully, to look more closely. The camera flashed.

"A piece of scalp is missing with hair attached, about two inches in diameter. The shape is precise. The cut was made very neatly, possibly with a scalpel. There are cuts to the face, particularly to the mouth. At each corner the blade has cut deep into the cheek and upwards towards the earlobe."

Greco looked down at his feet. Why do that? He pictured the killer insisting she smile, and when she didn't, or couldn't, he'd cut one into her face.

"The main wound on the torso is to the chest, at the site of the heart. It's deep and long but this isn't what killed her. The cause of death was the burning that occurred after the chest wall was cut into. It looks to me as if the cutting was to gain access."

"Bloody lunatic," Quickenden said, finally putting in an appearance.

"There is evidence of rape," Doctor Barrington continued. "There is extensive vaginal bruising, though I can't see any semen present."

"So he used a condom? Thoughtful of him," Quickenden said, shuffling from one foot to the other. Greco had noticed it was something he did when he was anxious.

"It would appear so. I'll take swabs to make sure. I'll be doing toxicology tests as well."

"Tortured and killed." Greco inhaled. "He took his time with her."

"It looks that way," the pathologist said.

Doctor Barrington took a scalpel and made the customary incision lengthways down the body. Her assistant held out a bowl.

Greco looked away.

"Her heart is extensively damaged. Access to the heart was made by a sharp blade. It entered the chest wall between the ribs. Your killer knew what he was doing. After the incision a long, thin object that had first been heated to a high temperature, was pushed deep into the heart muscle."

"The poker we found?" Greco asked.

"There is what looks like soot residue. Tests will confirm," the pathologist said. She was holding Jessie's heart in her hands. "The burning extends through the heart muscle and into the right ventricle."

"It's an odd way to kill someone," Greco said.

"Who knows what goes on in these people's heads, Inspector."

"About before, sir, not being here. It couldn't be helped," Quickenden interrupted.

"Later, Sergeant," Greco barked.

"That's about it," Natasha said. She looked up.

"I'll get everything processed and on the system as soon as," added one of the assistants. He was removing the hood of his coverall.

"You met Mark at the house," the pathologist said. "He and Roxy are the latest additions to the team here."

He nodded at the detectives.

The forensic scientist, Doctor Roxy Atkins, came up to Greco and Quickenden. She was young and petite. Her dark hair was cut short but a long fringe covered her forehead. She wore dark red lipstick and heavy black eyeliner. This, and her pale complexion, made her look slightly gothy.

"Like I said at the scene, her clothes were cut from her body. Also, a square of fabric has been neatly cut from her skirt. It's about two inches, the same as the cut on her scalp. It could be that your killer is collecting trophies," Atkins said.

Greco said nothing for a few seconds. He was hoping this wasn't the case, because it meant that they probably had a serial killer on their hands.

"Thank you. Useful information," he said.

Chapter 3

The main office was crowded. Greco's people were there — Grace, Jed Quickenden and DC Craig Merrick, and a couple of uniformed officers. DCI Colin Green and DI Westbury, who led the other team at the station, were also present.

Greco stood by the incident board. He pinned up the photo of Jessie Weston and wrote some notes. "You all know why we're here," he began. He looked round the room. He wished they would all sit down. It would have made the room look neater. Most were holding mugs of tea or coffee. Cups littered the desks. The untidiness of the room was disturbing his concentration. He had to get a grip on himself.

"Sir!" Quickenden approached the board. "It really wasn't my fault that I was late for the PM."

"Now isn't the time, Sergeant," Greco told him.

"It was the lad, Jonathan Weston," he continued. "He went to pieces. He was okay when I went to the flat, weirdly okay in fact, but when he saw her . . ." Quickenden shook his head. "It was like something took him over. It was all me and the uniform could do to hold him down."

"So what happened?" Greco asked, interested despite himself.

"He identified her, then he started to trash the place. He threw a chair across the room and attacked the mortuary attendant."

"You calmed him down though?"

"The Duggan security people took over. I had to leave them to it. I gave the PC the job of taking him home and came to join you."

"Sir!" DC Grace Harper interrupted. "I knew her."

"You knew the victim, Jessie Weston? Are you sure?"

"Yes, but I haven't spoken to her in a while. She wasn't one of my close friends or anything. We're the same age, both brought up on the Link. We used to go to the same school, Oldston Comp. If I saw her in a pub or round the town, we'd speak, have a quick update, but that's all."

"When did you last speak to her?"

"It's got to be last summer," Grace Harper replied. "She was in the park when I was there with Holly. But I do know that in recent times she had a boyfriend."

"That could be the young man in the photo." Greco tapped it. "Do you want to give us a quick background report? It would be useful."

Of the three of them — she, Quickenden and Merrick, Grace was the brightest. She was also the most ambitious. She was held back because she was a single parent, with all the childcare problems that came along with it. Greco had come to appreciate her situation in recent times.

He rapped on the desk in front of him.

"You all know what's happened," he began. "The PM report, bar toxicology, will be on the system later today." He looked at Georgina Booth, the station's information officer, known to everyone as George. "You will all liaise with Georgina with regard to HOLMES. Each of you will enter everything you get individually, and George will produce consolidated reports on a daily basis. Are you okay with that?"

George nodded.

"For the duration of the case, Georgina will be assigned exclusively to your team," DCI Green said.

That was something at least. George was good at what she did, but usually she was shared between the different teams. It was more cost-cutting that Greco didn't approve of. He knew she would appreciate having a larger role in the investigation.

"It's important that we all get acquainted with Jessie Weston's world quickly," Greco told them. "Grace knew her, so she will give us the benefit of a background briefing." He smiled at the DC, and moved aside. She was wearing her long blonde hair loose today. It softened her appearance and bobbed on her shoulders as she walked. Grace Harper was still only in her twenties, but her life had been hard. It showed in her face. Scraping her long hair back into a ponytail, the way she usually wore it, did little for her.

"I didn't know her well, not recently. It was more a school thing. Jessie came from a difficult family. Like most folk on the Link, the Westons had little money and the kids' father did a runner early on. Mark, her brother, has been in bother numerous times for shoplifting and burglary. He's not all there," she said, looking at Speedy, "which was why he'll have kicked off at the mortuary. Mavis Weston, their mother, is something else though. She's a real force to be reckoned with. Back in the day, all the kids on the Link were terrified of her, me included. But she did love her own kids, and neither of them has left home yet. Jessie's had lots of jobs, but recently she worked at the Crown Inn. I've seen her there a couple of times. She did a few night shifts and all the lunchtimes. People liked her, she was a good laugh."

"Tell us about the boyfriend," Greco prompted.

"There was a rumour a few months ago that she was going out with Frankie Farr. You know, of Farr Construction fame, that bloke who's always shoving up houses around here. I found it hard to believe because they're just so different." She paused. "Jessie was okay in her own environment, but she's leagues away from the world Frankie moves in. He's got money for a start. But the rumours were true. They were seen in the Crown, sat together in a corner, kissing and canoodling."

"Why were you so surprised?" Greco asked.

"To put it bluntly, Jessie was dead common. She wouldn't take offence either, if you said it to her. She knew what she looked like. She wore short skirts, low slung tops and flirted with anything in trousers — and not just flirting either. She got pregnant at fifteen. That resulted in one abortion, and I was told there were others since."

"And Frankie Farr?"

"He's from a close family. He's an only child and a self-made business man. He's a good-looking guy who could have anyone he wanted. So it always puzzled me why he chose to go around with Jessie of all people."

"In that case we'll be sure to ask him," Greco said. "Thanks, Grace. That was very useful. It gives us a flavour of the girl."

"Have we made arrangements for family liaison to keep an eye on the Westons?" DCI Green asked.

"Yes, sir. I contacted them when DS Quickenden was taking Jonathan to the Duggan," George told them.

"I don't fancy their chances, whoever it is. Mavis will eat them alive," said Grace.

Greco tapped on the desk top. "Back to the investigation. We need to know what Jessie was up to yesterday. Last night is particularly important. Where had she been? Had she been working? If not, who'd she been with? What was she doing on Arnold Street? It's in the opposite direction from the Link, where she lived. It was late, so where was she going? Had she upset someone? So far we have no obvious motive for such a horrific killing. It was premeditated and he was waiting for her. The man who killed her had time to light a fire, don't forget."

"My guess is she'd been working," Quickenden offered.

"We don't guess," Greco said.

"We don't know that the killer was targeting Jessie," said Grace. "There is always the possibility that if this was the work of some nutcase, then any young woman walking down that road last night would've been a target."

"Grace has a point. So keep an open mind. Grace and I will follow up on Jessie's activities yesterday, but it's important to look at that house, and the street as well," he said. "The house she was found in is up for sale. Craig . . ." he said to DC Craig Merrick. "You and Quickenden will speak to the estate agents, Harvey & Son, in Oldston Centre. Who has been to view or shown an interest in the property recently? Find the owner and speak to him. Go down that street and speak to the neighbours. But be careful. Ask but don't give anything away. We don't want to reveal any of the details. Jessie was murdered, and that's as far as we go. The press have already got hold of this. Once they smell the truth about what's happened, we'll not get rid of them. While you're talking to the neighbours, find out who'd lived in that house previously. It looked as if it was being refurbished. Someone else may have had a key — a workman, a friend, or a neighbour."

They looked serious and businesslike, and were all taking notes. The team had come a long way since their first case together. Except for Quickenden. He was standing by the window, his attention on something going on outside. Greco looked at him.

"There's a bunch of reporters out there now, sir," he said. "I spotted Laycock from the *Herald*, and that chap from the Manchester paper has joined him. The rest are from the smaller, local papers. No TV or radio yet, thank goodness."

"We ignore them. We'll hold a press conference when we're ready."

"I'll have a word," DCI Green said. "Fob them off for now."

"We need to get on with this quickly. Back here at five to collate what we've got," said Greco.

* * *

Grace was pleased the inspector had chosen her and not Speedy to join him. That would be down to her having known Jessie. She was under no illusions that it was anything else. Greco was no womaniser. He was back with his ex-wife and seemed happier. He was certainly a lot easier to work with nowadays. It was a shame though. He was the type of man women drooled over, and Grace was no exception. She doubted he was even aware of it.

"You did well during the briefing," he said as they went out. "That point about not targeting Jessie specifically, is a valid one. But if that is the case, then you know what it means?"

"Yes, sir. Like I said in there, we could be dealing with a psycho."

"I sincerely hope not. If we are, then no woman in this town is safe until he's caught."

The minute they walked out of the door, the reporters were upon them. The questions came thick and fast. Cameras flashed and several pushed voice recorders in their faces.

"Got any suspects?" a voice called out. "What was done to her? Bad, I've heard."

"Ignore them," Greco muttered. He ushered Grace towards a car.

"You have to give us something, Inspector, or this lot will make it up!"

This was Oliver Laycock from the *Oldston Herald*. Grace recognised him from the photo on his weekly column. He was somewhere in his mid-forties, tall with black hair and a short cropped beard.

"I would suggest you don't do that, Mr Laycock," Greco said, and stopped in front of him.

Laycock grinned at Greco. He moved aside to let a dark-haired female photographer through.

"Smile, Inspector! I'm sure my readers would like a picture. You're very photogenic for a cop."

Inside the car, Grace locked the door and started the engine. That reporter had got it right, whoever she was. As she prepared to move away, the camera was still flashing, and it wasn't flashing at Grace. Before he'd patched things up with Suzy, Grace had hoped that she and Greco might get close. She'd dropped enough hints. She'd even helped him with childcare when Suzy had dumped his little girl on him. He'd been grateful, and it had changed their relationship, but not in the way she'd hoped. He was more open, less standoffish with her. But, wife or not, the more Grace got to know him, the more she realised that there was never going to be anything between them. Greco didn't mix work and pleasure. He kept all his colleagues at arm's length and only rarely joined them for a drink in the pub.

Grace pulled away, heading towards the centre of town. The female photographer kept flashing away at them. "She likes you," Grace joked.

"She wants a story, that's all."

"She said you were photogenic."

"Like I said, a story. And if she thinks a bit of flattery will get her anywhere, she's very wrong."

"There's nothing wrong with flirting, sir." Grace bit her tongue. Why did she have to say that?

"There is when you're a married man. And anyway, reporters aren't my cup of tea." He chuckled.

Grace felt her cheeks flush. "Sorry, sir. Slip of the tongue. I didn't mean anything by it. But you're not actually married, are you? You and Suzy are divorced."

"A formality," he assured her. "We will put things right very soon."

Amazing. He hadn't shut her out. He didn't seem to mind talking about his family with her. With everyone else it was very much a no go area.

"The press are really going to make this difficult," he said, looking into the rear mirror. "You recognised Laycock?"

"Only from his column. Some of the stuff he writes makes my blood boil, but I've never had a run in with him before."

"I think we're being followed."

"The red saloon? I spotted it. I'll try and lose it. I'll take a run up the bypass first, put them off the scent. Then I thought the Crown? Speak to the staff. Check what shifts Jessie worked yesterday, and what time she left."

"My thoughts too," he said. "After which, I suppose we'll have to speak to her mother."

"God help us. Mavis won't be pleased. She hates the police, and given what's happened she's bound to blame us," Grace replied.

"That's hardly logical."

"Mavis isn't logical. She'll be emotional and angry and she'll want to vent that anger on someone."

Grace took them down the bypass towards Manchester and then around the first roundabout. By the time they were back in Oldston, the red saloon had disappeared.

"The Crown has a car park but I'll hide ours round the back," she said.

"What's this place like?"

"I've not been here in a while. You know how it is, getting babysitters and all that. The last time I came here they were doing meals. The food wasn't bad either."

"Me and Suzy could do with finding somewhere local and decent to eat."

"Hope you have better luck than I did. I was halfway through the pudding when I got a phone call to say that Holly had a temperature." She rolled her eyes. "I haven't bothered much since then."

"Who runs this place?"

"A woman called Megan Hunter. She's okay, doesn't stand for any bother. She's a friend of my mother's."

It was three in the afternoon and, apart from a couple finishing a late lunch, the pub was empty.

Grace spoke to the woman behind the bar. "DC Harper and DI Greco. Oldston CID."

"Jessie?" The woman's face dropped. "I can't get my head round it. She was only here last night, stood where you are now," she said, nodding at Greco.

"Are you Megan Hunter?" said Greco.

"Yes. I'm the landlady." She beamed at Grace. "You okay, Grace? Enjoying the job?"

Grace smiled back, and nodded. "What hours did Jessie work yesterday?"

"She did the lunchtime shift, twelve to four. She was back in at nine and stayed until eleven thirty. She was fine, laughing and chatting with the punters. There were no problems, nothing unusual. I just don't get it."

"Did she leave with anyone?" Greco asked.

"No. She did tell me earlier on that Frankie was picking her up, but then she got a text. Apparently he couldn't make it. Had a better offer, if you ask me."

Megan Hunter folded her arms and tucked them under her chest.

"I take it you don't like him much?" Grace said.

"He's flash and mouthy. He looks like class but that's a sham, believe me. I don't care what school he went to or how wealthy his family is — that young man is trouble."

"Anything in particular?" Grace said.

"He started a fight in here last weekend, all over nothing. Some bloke slapped Jessie on the backside and he was off. Jumped over the table and wrestled him to the floor."

Grace shot Greco a look. This was a side of Frankie Farr she hadn't known about.

"He might look like a well-mannered, businessman type, but that's just the gloss. I think that's why he liked Jessie so much. He recognised a kindred spirit. With her he could be himself, act natural. He didn't have to put on that front of his." Megan Hunter winked. "The one with you looks okay, Grace. Your mother would approve."

Grace blushed. God knows what Greco must think. They weren't here for a drink, for pity's sake. They were investigating a murder. "Did Frankie Farr come in here at all yesterday?" she said.

"Not as I remember." Megan paused. "No. Last time he was in was the night before. And that night he took Jessie home. She came into work yesterday, so everything must have been fine."

"Did Jessie spend time with anyone else yesterday? Did anyone bother her last night? Ask to meet up after her shift?"

"No, I don't think so. We were run off our feet to be honest. Oldston United were playing at home and the ground is only down the road."

"Thanks, Megan. You've been a help. We might need to talk to you again though." Grace smiled.
"Come back anytime. And bring your dishy bloke with you!" They returned to the car.

Grace was blushing again. "Sorry about that, sir."

"It's okay, Grace."

"What do you think? What she said about Frankie Farr — that's not how I saw him at all," said Grace.

"Megan Hunter has no reason to lie, and she sees more of him than you do. We'll speak to him, and see what we think. Jessie's movements yesterday seem straightforward enough. But if she wasn't seeing Frankie and she wasn't going home, then what was she doing on Arnold Street?"

"Even if Megan Hunter didn't hear it, Jessie could have arranged to meet someone. Like I said at the briefing, Jessie was a bit of a man-eater. Anything in trousers . . ."

"Is it likely, given she had Frankie Farr on her case?"

"With the Jessie I knew, highly likely. She had precious few scruples and wouldn't think twice if the offer was good enough."

"Fancy tackling Mavis now?"

"We'll go to the flat, and see if she's back yet. If she isn't, then we'd better find Frankie Farr. See what he's got to say for himself."

Chapter 4

Something bad, something bad.

What did they mean, those words going round in his head? They were making him feel dizzy. *He* wasn't helping by shaking that cereal into a bowl. If *he* thinks I can eat breakfast, *he's* bloody mad!

"Help yourself to milk."

"Was I here last night? I can't remember."

The man laughed, and carried on sorting breakfast. *He* shouldn't laugh. It was getting him confused. Neville didn't know what was funny anymore. He still hadn't worked out if this man was real. He looked real, but then they all did. His world was populated by shadowy figures — some spoke, some didn't. Some said they would help him . . . all this one did was give him pills.

Neville stared at him, trying to work it out. Could he trust his own mind? Well, the short answer to that was *no*. He wanted to reach out and grab hold of *him*, touch real flesh. The urge made his palms itch. But he was scared. What if *he* wasn't real? What then? Neville didn't even know *his* name. He didn't even know when *he'd* appeared in his life, or how.

"I'm surprised you need to ask that."

"The voices were playing up again. They were at me all night. They wanted me to do something bad." Neville lowered his voice. "I *have* done something bad. I must have done. They don't give up, those voices. If I don't do what they want, they don't go away. They bellow away inside here." He pointed to his head.

"You had a good time, though. Didn't I say we'd have fun?"

"When was that?"

"A while ago."

"It was bad fun. I hurt that girl."

"Make sure you take your pills properly today."

"What good will they do?" Does *he* really think they do any good? "You do believe me. I'm not telling lies. I went somewhere last night and I did something real bad."

He had that look on his face. "You know, don't you? You know what I did."

"Yes, I know," *he* said at last.

The relief. Neville closed his eyes and lets it wash through him. It wasn't a dream. It was real. *He* was real — the man. Neville had done those things. He remembered now. He wasn't going mad after all.

"You're all over the papers." The man slapped down the latest edition of the *Herald* on the table. "You're famous. You, of all people. Imagine that."

"Will I like being famous?" Neville wasn't sure. Could a person be famous for doing those bad things?

"Depends whether they catch you or not."

Neville tried to read what it said. But the words moved and blurred in front of his eyes. "They haven't put my name. Shall I tell them?"

The man looks at him steadily. It made Neville nervous.

"Not yet. Better keep quiet for now. You haven't told anyone else, have you?"

"No. Only you. I trust you."

"Trust." *He* pulled a face. "Dangerous that. You shouldn't trust anyone."

"I want to do it again. The voice keeps telling me to. It never stops. It's in here all the time." Neville banged his head with the flat of his hand. "Will you sort it?" He smiled at the man. "You know about that too, don't you? You know I can't stop."

"What did you do to that girl, Neville?"

"I hurt her. I hurt her bad and I . . . you know." He sniggered. "She had no clothes on. I couldn't help it."

"I said I'd give you a girl of your own. Stick with me. I keep my promises." *He* clapped Neville on the back. "But you did more than hurt her. She's dead, according to the papers."

"I didn't want to kill her. Just her heart. The voice said she'd never love me. I had to do something. The voice wouldn't let up. It kept on and on about how she'd leave me. How she'd go off with someone else. I couldn't let her cheat on me. She'd make me unhappy. I had to do it."

"Kill a heart, you kill a person. That's how it works, Neville."

"I didn't know."

"What are you doing today?"

"Are you going to take me out?"

"No. I've got to work. You should stay here. Stay inside and don't speak to anyone."

"Will they come and take me away?"

"Not if you keep your head down."

"I want to see Edna. She makes me feel safe. Edna will know what to do."

"Bad idea."

"The voices say I must. She'll know what to do. That's what the voices say."

"Sod the voices! I'm telling you to stay in and lock the doors. If you don't do as I say, I'll shop you to the bloody police myself."

* * *

"What's with the boss taking Grace and not you?" DC Craig Merrick asked Speedy.

"Don't give a toss what he does. The less I have to do the better, mate, especially with him. I'm sick of the job to be honest."

Jed Quickenden had been at the briefing but he'd hardly heard a word. He had paid attention only to Grace. He'd been lusting after her for months, but she completely ignored him.

"Come off it, Speedy, you don't mean that. People will forget the Geegee business and things will settle down, you'll see."

"If there's one thing I know about the folk around here it's that they've got long memories. No one is ever going to trust me again. I grew up in this town, now half of it avoids me."

"They don't like me much either." Merrick grinned.

He knew that the younger man looked up to him for some reason. "That's because you're a copper, stupid," said Quickenden, slapping the back of Merrick's head. "They didn't mind me because I used to be like them, a bad boy. Now I'll be lucky to reach my next birthday."

"Don't be daft. No one would dare do you any harm. Grady Gibbs wasn't that powerful. He had his enemies too."

"Then there's all the other people who were upset — the Hussains for a start. They won't be best pleased now their lucrative little import business has been snatched away."

"You need to chill, get your head together. You've got time owing, take it. Get away somewhere hot."

"Greco will never allow that."

"Go above his head. Ask Green. Tell him how you feel."

"He'll think I've gone soft."

"If you ask me, that's exactly what's happened," Merrick said. They were pulling into the shopping centre car park in Oldston.

"Don't you go saying anything." Speedy poked his arm. "I've got enough on my plate without Greco on my case."

"Harvey & Sons are over there."

"Better get this over with," said Quickenden.

Andrew Harvey, the owner, was a small, bald man wearing round glasses. He flitted about the office, tweaking pictures of houses and straightening piles of brochures while he talked.

"I've had the owner in. Shocked he was. He saw her, you know. Said it was a sight he'd never forget. Dreadful, was how he described it."

"We need to know who has viewed the place — say in the last month," Speedy said.

"That's easy. No one," said Harvey. "It needs far too much work. It's riddled with damp and needs a complete rewire. The whole street should be pulled down and rebuilt. None of the sales on that street have gone through. Once a surveyor's had a look, the price drops like a stone. That one, number eight, needs a shedload of work and the owner won't listen."

"So there's been no one at all, not even an enquiry?" Speedy said.

"I'll check, but I'm fairly sure."

He sat at his desk and accessed a file on his computer. "Asking far too much and won't drop. With all that work required — well." Harvey held out his arms, palm up. "I have told Mr Rahman, but he's adamant."

"Can I have the owner's address, please?" Speedy said.

"I shouldn't, not really."

"We are police officers. We can find out by other means, but it would save us some time."

Harvey shrugged and sent the information to the printer. "Here you are, but you'll be lucky to find him. He got a shock yesterday and I believe he's gone to see relatives in Birmingham. He's left the keys with me."

"Who has access to them?"

"We keep all the vendors' keys in the safe, Sergeant. If there's an enquiry, then one of us takes them to do the viewing. But like I said, there's been no one."

"And keys to the safe?"

"Only me."

"If anyone does enquire about the house, you will let us know?" Speedy handed him his card and they left.

"Looks like we need to knock on a few doors," Merrick said.

"What's the betting that'll be a waste of time too?"

"Whoever did this isn't invisible, Speedy. He'll have made a mistake somewhere along the line. All we have to do is find it."

"You sound more like him every bloody day." Speedy turned and walked back to the car.

* * *

"It's a long way up," Grace said. "Twelfth floor, and a half-hearted lift."

"I think I'm fit enough to make it," Greco said sarcastically.

"Do you still run?"

"Try to. Apart from the exercise being good, it clears my head."

"Wish I could find something that cleared mine. I do the job all day and see to Holly most of the night. She's not sleeping well at the moment. She keeps having nightmares."

"Matilda sleeps like a log, always has. Suzy says she's the only child she knows who actually asks to go to bed."

"You're very lucky."

"Suppose I am. I don't realise it half the time," he said, smiling.

Up on the twelfth floor, Greco banged on the Westons' door. There was no answer. Grace peered through the dirty window.

A woman stuck her head out of the next door along. "None of them are in. He went out earlier, with the cops I think, and he hasn't come back. She's been gone most of the week and Jessie will be working."

So the news hadn't reached the Link yet.

"If Mrs Weston comes back, would you ask her to ring us, please?" Grace handed the woman a card.

"Best of luck with that one, love," said the neighbour, and went back inside.

"What now, sir?"

"We'd better go and talk to Frankie Farr."

Grace drove out to Farr Construction. The builders' yard and offices were in a new industrial estate on the outskirts of Oldston.

"Is Mr Farr in?" Grace showed her badge to the receptionist. "DI Greco and DC Harper from Oldston CID."

The woman eyed them suspiciously from behind her desk. "Is this about the car?"

"No," Greco said. "Why? Has something happened?"

"It was stolen. Last night. Young Mr Farr's pride and joy. He's gutted."

"Is he here?"

She got up and knocked on a door to one side of the reception desk. They were admitted straight away.

"Found my car?" Farr said.

He was tall, good-looking and dressed in a designer suit. Grace guessed he must be about her own age. He had jet black hair and was clean shaven. His nose was slightly misshapen. It must have been broken at some time. Grace wondered if it was a sporting injury or perhaps it had happened in a fight. Maybe there was something to what Megan Hunter had told them.

"We're here about Jessie, Mr Farr."

"Well, *she* didn't take the thing." He walked over to the window. "It should be parked right there. Some bastard's going to suffer for this. That car cost me a fortune."

"Mr Farr, Jessie has been murdered," Grace said. "Sometime last night, after she finished work at the Crown."

He spun round and stared at them. His mouth hung open, and his dark eyes narrowed almost to pinpricks. "You're joking!"

Greco shook his head. "Sadly not. She was murdered."

"That can't be right. Who'd want to murder Jessie?"

"Did you see her at any time yesterday?" Grace said.

Frankie Farr took a bottle of brandy from a cupboard. He poured a generous slug into a glass, and then sat down. He looked close to tears. "I couldn't. I had meetings all day. Last night I had to go to a family thing. My mother's birthday, so I couldn't pick her up."

"Did you usually pick her up?"

"Whenever I could. I have a flat in that new block by the canal. Jessie liked it there, so she often stayed over. I wanted her to move in properly, but she wouldn't leave her brother."

"Did you text her or phone?" Grace said.

"We texted all the time." He gulped down the brandy. "She said it was what got her through the day. Well, me too, if I'm honest."

"Did she seem upset about anything? Did she say if anything was bothering her?" Grace said.

"She was pissed off with the new rota at work. Megan, the landlady, wanted her to do more nights. Jessie wasn't up for it, but that bitch was coming down hard on her. Threatened to get rid and find someone else if she didn't agree."

Grace and Greco looked at each other. Megan Hunter had not mentioned this.

"Did they argue about it?" Grace asked.

"They had a blazing row yesterday lunchtime. Jessie sent me a text." He took out his phone and went to the message. "See? She's going on about how unfair it all was and how Megan was picking on her."

"I see. And did this continue into last night's shift?"

"I don't think so. But I don't know what they sorted because I didn't talk or text Jess last night. I was with my family at some eatery up the hills — The Pennine Alehouse. There's no signal there so we were out of contact all night. When I got back to my flat it was gone one in the morning. I sent her a goodnight text, but got no reply."

"Thank you, Mr Farr," Greco said. "Here's my card. If anything happens, anyone contacts you or you remember something then call me." He paused. "Another thing. The press will most likely be in touch. My advice is to say nothing. They will pester you. They'll be saying things, most of which won't be true. Keep well away. They just want a story. They are not interested in catching Jessie's killer, only in having good copy to put in the papers."

Farr nodded. He was pouring more brandy as they left the room.

"I don't think he's taken it in, not really," Grace said. "He looked devastated."

"He didn't ask though, did he?"

"Ask what?"

"How she died. What was done to her. But he was very keen to tell us about the argument Jessie had with Megan at the pub. Check that one out. See what Megan has to say."

* * *

38

Craig Merrick had been knocking at the house next to where the murder had taken place. He caught up with Speedy, who was further along the road.

"No one in."

"Nobody along here is going to tell us anything," Speedy said. He banged on a door further down the street. "Tight-lipped so and sos, the bloody lot of them."

A middle-aged woman answered. She had her hair in curlers. "We're investigating the murder that took place up the street," Merrick said, flashing his badge. "Did you see or hear anything unusual last night?"

"I heard nowt, love. Too busy watching the box. My husband's deaf so we have it turned up loud. I heard the police cars though, early on this morning."

"Did you know the people who used to live there?" Speedy asked.

"Old Mrs Baxter. She lived there most of her life. She's in a care home now I think — if she's still alive."

"Did she sell to Mr Rahman?"

"No, he's always owned it. He owns a lot of them along here. Mrs Baxter rented from him."

"Have the press been round at all?" Merrick asked.

"Camped out on that corner all morning. Asked all sorts of questions. Don't think they got owt though. No one knows owt, you see."

"Thanks." Merrick handed her a card. "If you think of anything else, give us a ring."

Speedy was already off, back down the street. "There is someone in. I just saw the curtains twitch." He banged on the neighbouring door again, and eventually a man answered.

"I've nothing more to say. I told you people everything this morning."

"What people, Mr . . . ?"

"Ernest Talbot. You lot. You were all over the street earlier. Cameras, the lot."

"Not us, Mr Talbot. We're the police," Speedy said. "We're DC Merrick and DS Quickenden from Oldston CID."

"What did you tell the papers?" Merrick said.

"Look, I'm on short time at work and they said they'd pay for anything I could give them. I'd be stupid not to, wouldn't I?"

"Did you go in there last night?"

"No. Rahman wouldn't let me. He said it was dreadful what had happened to that poor girl. He said I didn't want that picture in my head."

"He did you a favour." Speedy spoke with feeling. Whenever he closed his eyes, the image came back to him. "So if you didn't go in, how come you were so helpful to the press?"

Ernest Talbot shrugged. "Rahman let one or two details slip. And I've got an imagination, haven't I? Anyway, they don't care what they write."

Speedy took out his notebook. "What did you actually see?"

"Nowt. I was in bed."

"Did you hear anything?" This was painful.

"A scream — I think. It's what woke me up. I live on my own, well, me and the cat. Bloodcurdling it was. You know, the kind of thing you get in horror films. I woke up and listened for a bit but it went quiet. Then I heard something else, talking it sounded like, coming from Rahman's place. There shouldn't have been anyone there. It's up for sale and empty. I took a look out the window and saw the smoke. That chimney needs a bloody good sweep. The smoke was all over the street."

"So you rang Mr Rahman?"

"Yes, I did. Two in the morning or not, he needed to know. I thought he had squatters."

"Don't say another word to the press, or anyone else," Speedy said. "I want you to come into the station tomorrow and give a formal statement. Have a think, and write down anything you remember about last night. Anything at all."

Chapter 5

"I know it's late, but can we feedback on what we've got so far?" Greco said. He'd seen Grace eyeing the office clock and understood that she needed to get away. "All Grace and I got was a bit of a mismatch in the stories of the landlady of the Crown and Frankie Farr. We'll check it out tomorrow. What about you, Speedy? What did you and Merrick glean from the residents of Arnold Street?"

"Ernest Talbot, the neighbour, is a tricky one. He's already spoken to the press and reckons he told them a lot of rubbish, but he could be lying. But he did alert Rahman, and he says he heard a scream."

"Is that it? No one see a car? A stranger? Anything odd? Did anyone even see Jessie on that street? Do we even know what she was doing there?"

"She was going to see Ethel Ridley, my mother!" A woman spoke from the doorway. Her voice was angry.

They all turned towards the door.

"Mavis Weston." Grace grimaced.

The woman looked at each of them, finally settling on Greco. "Have you found him yet? That murdering bastard needs stringing up too. He needs to get a taste of what he dishes out."

The comment bothered Greco. She'd made a direct reference to how Jessie had been found. What exactly did she know and, more to the point, who had told her?

"Mrs Weston, we are investigating, but its early days," he said.

"Not good enough. You need to up your game, copper. He's a bad 'un. He needs catching and dealing with. If you don't do it, I know some who will."

Her face was full of hate. Her eyes went from one team member to another.

"We are putting every resource into this," he said.

"That man murdered my girl. He wasn't kind. He didn't just bash her over the head and have done with it," she said.

Her eyes were blazing. She was barely keeping it together. Someone had told her. The press?

"Who have you been talking to, Mrs Weston?"

"I have every right to know how my daughter died," she said. "I know things because I keep my ears open. Shame you lot don't do the same."

Her eyes were everywhere, all over the team — and the room. At last they found the incident board. She gave a strangled cry. "They said . . . but I didn't believe it. What did that monster do to my girl?"

Greco stood in her path to prevent her from going any closer. "Come with me," he said. "We'll go somewhere and talk. Craig, arrange some tea, would you?"

He took her along the corridor to an empty office. It had a leather sofa against the wall. He gestured for her to sit down. "We have been trying to find you. We needed to get Jessie identified quickly so that the investigation can get off the ground."

"So that you can cut her to pieces, you mean. I know what goes on." She took a breath and wiped the tears from her eyes. "You shouldn't have asked Mark. He can't hack it. He comes across as gobby, but he's a sensitive lad."

Mavis Weston was weeping openly now, a hankie clutched to her face. Greco felt sorry for the woman. She'd just lost her daughter in dreadful circumstances. It was enough to make the toughest person crumble.

"I want to see her," she said finally.

"That can be arranged. Let me have a word with the doctors first."

"The heartless sods have butchered her, haven't they? Cut her to pieces and sewed her back together all wrong."

"It really isn't like that," he said. "But there are certain things that have to be done, evidence that has to be gathered . . . Are you up to answering some questions?"

She looked at him. Every battle she'd ever fought was etched into her face. Mavis Weston was a tough woman. She was dressed in jeans and a shirt. They were nothing special, cheap market-bought clothing. Her hair was a patchwork of different colours, as if she couldn't make up her mind which one she preferred. But the truth was there, in the inch or so of grey at the roots.

"What d'you want to know, copper?"

"When did you last see Jessie?"

"Over a week ago. The Saturday before last. I've been to my sister's in Barnsley. Me and Jessie, we spoke on the phone and she texted me, but not much, not like usual. We'd had words. I wanted her to stay at home and take care of Jonno but she didn't want to. She was spending more and more time with that lad of hers, Frankie Farr. Jonno's no good on his own. He can't cope."

"You said she was going to your mother's last night. Where does she live?"

"She's in the care home by the park. Arnold Street is a short cut, that's why Jessie would go that way. God knows why she had to visit at that time of night though. You'll have to ask at the home. If that bitch that runs the pub had let her go on time she might even be alive now. Treated our Jess like a bloody slave she did."

44

Another reference to Megan Hunter. She was beginning to look like a less than perfect employer.

"Was there a problem with your mother?"

"No idea. I haven't spoken to the woman in nearly twenty years. If there was a problem, they wouldn't ring me. Jessie was the emergency contact."

"My sergeant went round to your flat. Jonathan didn't know where you were."

"He's as daft as a brush. I rang him every day, but he forgets. He spends all night boozing and watching football, his brains addled."

Craig brought the tea in and handed them each a mug. Mavis eyed the young constable.

"They keep getting younger." She shook her head. "I hope you've got more clout behind this case than the likes of that pretty boy there."

"Constable Merrick is okay. He does a good job."

"He's a bloody kid. I want this one caught, Inspector. So don't piss about."

"He's young, but he has experience and a good team to work with. We will do our best, Mrs Weston, I assure you."

"Make sure you do."

"Generally speaking, did you and Jessie get on?"

"We had our moments. She could be a right cow. Jessie was a difficult child. She always went her own way and she never changed. When it came to it, she'd always choose her latest man over the family. I suppose I can't blame her. I used to be the same. I dragged them kids up on my own. Got no help from their father, and I had to work long hours. The kids were left to their own devices and it didn't do either of them any good."

"Does her father know?"

"No idea. Probably not. I was never married to him. When he buggered off I changed my name by deed poll, so it was the same as the kids.'" She put the empty mug on the window sill.

"What's his name, Jessie's dad?"

"Eric Weston. Last I heard he was living Stockport way."

Greco jotted the name down.

"You get the bastard that did for my girl and make it quick. I want him to pay. My Jessie wasn't perfect but she didn't deserve to die, not like that." Mavis stood up.

"I can have someone stay with you — a family liaison officer," Greco said.

"Police? Staying with me? You're having a laugh. I don't want any of you round my place frightening Mark. None of you. Got that? Ring me and I'll come in if you've any information."

"Okay, we'll stay in touch."

"She was so even-tempered it was scary," Grace remarked, once she'd gone. "I didn't hear any shouting at all."

"She's hurting. However tough she is, Mavis is Jessie's mother," he said. "Where are the others?"

"Speedy's done one and Craig's gone to get something to eat. He reckons he'll put what they got today onto HOLMES before he leaves."

"What is it with Speedy at the moment? He's obviously got something on his mind."

"He's not been right since Grady Gibbs was killed. He's got it in his head that people blame him. He doesn't feel that he fits in anywhere anymore, not here and not with his old mates in the town either."

"If Speedy doesn't fit in, what about me?"

Grace smiled reassuringly. "You're doing okay, sir. The others are used to you now."

"Should I offer to help?"

"He's best left. He reckons he's been through the mincer these last months. He'll come round in his own good time."

* * *

46

"You're late again. Matilda is up in her room getting ready for bed."

"Couldn't be helped, Suzy. Work stuff. We've got a killer to find and he's not making things easy for us." With a sigh, Greco flopped down into an armchair. "In fact, if forensics doesn't come up with anything, we're really going to struggle."

Suzy Greco shook her head. "Despite what you've said, crime is worse here. You seem to have tons more to do. You're run ragged and it shows." She brushed back the hair that had fallen onto his forehead. "How are that team of yours shaping up? Any better?"

What to tell her? He wasn't sure he knew himself. Grace was okay, but as for Speedy and Merrick . . .

"Speedy's going through some sort of crisis apparently. He's told Grace he doesn't fit in anymore."

"I thought that was your thing, not fitting in." She chuckled. "So what's wrong with him?"

"He's not happy. But I'd guessed that much already. He isn't interested in anything that's going on. Problem is — he's my sergeant and I need him."

"What about Grace? You keep saying how good she is."

"She is. She's outperforming him at the moment. But she's still only a DC. Speedy has to shoulder more of the responsibility. He should be capable of much more. He was excellent once — before I came here."

"What are you going to do about it?"

"I've got no idea. I spoke to Grace and she says it'll pass and to wait it out. But it's a situation I can do without at the moment. This case we're working on is hard enough without Speedy going all weird on me."

"Try to be more of a people person, Stephen. It'd help if your team could come to you with their work problems."

A people person. In Greco's opinion you either were or you weren't. Suzy was. She got on with her colleagues at the college and with the students. She had a great personality. She smiled a lot and she was pretty. Suzy Greco had a lot going for her. But he wasn't like that.

"Matilda's got a new friend. I've said she can have her round for tea one day this week. Think you'll be able to join us?"

"I'll try. Is she asleep yet?"

"I think she's seeing to Mortimer."

"Who's Mortimer? A new teddy?"

"Not exactly. Matilda had a particularly good day at school, so she got to bring him home as a treat."

"I'll go and help her." Greco pushed his weary frame from the comfort of the chair and went upstairs to be with his daughter.

"Tillyflop!" he called out. She rushed to greet him.

"Come and see Mortimer!" She took his hand and dragged him excitedly into her room. "He's a hamster."

Greco gave a shudder. A *hamster*. And in her bedroom too. "Shouldn't he be downstairs?" That creature should be outside in the garage. He didn't even want to think about the germs, the dirt . . .

"No, he likes it with me. He's playing in his wheel."

"Don't put your fingers in there, will you? Those things bite."

"Mortimer doesn't, he's nice. He plays out in the classroom and he doesn't run away."

"You mustn't let him out in the house." His daughter screwed up her face. "He'll get lost," he added quickly. "He doesn't know his way around yet."

Matilda nodded.

"Make sure you wash your hands too," Greco said. "And stick his cage on the window sill over there."

"I want him next to me," she said with a frown. "Mummy said I could. *And* she said you'd make a fuss."

He ruffled her blonde hair. "Okay, Tillyflop. I give up."

He walked across the landing to the bathroom and gave his hands a scrub. It might look cute to Matilda, but all he could see was a fluffy rat.

"Don't start, Stephen. She's thrilled to bits," Suzy said as he returned to the kitchen. "Matilda's been waiting ages for her turn with Mortimer."

"Did I say anything?"

"You didn't have to."

"My cleaning lady is giving up," he told her. "It got me thinking. I should sell the flat. Spend the money on this place, or even somewhere new for all of us. What do you think?"

"If that's what you want to do. But don't feel that I'm forcing your hand," she said, and kissed his cheek.

"Perhaps a better idea would be to buy a house together, instead of paying rent," he said.

"It's an idea." She didn't sound enthusiastic and it surprised him.

"You're obviously not keen. I can't for the life of me see why not. I thought that was what we wanted — a new start, a new house, to cement everything together."

"It's not bricks and mortar that keeps relationships going, Stephen."

What was he not seeing?

"I'm not sure. Let's just wait and see," she said.

"Wait for what? What are we doing, Suzy? Are we a couple or not?"

The look on Suzy's face was evasive.

"Of course we're a couple, like we wanted." She was twirling her blonde hair through her fingers, like she did whenever she was nervous. "But it's early days. Maybe we should give things a bit longer. Make sure we're doing the right thing."

"It feels right to me. I don't see any point in waiting."

"Don't push it, Stephen. I like things the way they are."

49

"We're no longer married. Don't you want to put that right?"

She shrugged. "Is it that important? We're happy enough. Why spoil it?"

"Marriage won't spoil anything. And I'd like things to be right. If we're staying together, then we should make it official," he said.

"What would that achieve? I don't see that it makes any difference if we're married or not. We tried that once and it didn't work. This is far better if you ask me."

"In what way better? I don't understand why you want to hold back. If we got remarried it would put our relationship on a more secure footing."

"So you're insecure." She stood facing him, her hands on her hips. "Stephen, leave it. Things are fine. We're fine and, more to the point, Matilda is happy."

"Okay. If that's what you want."

"Yes it is." There was an edge to her voice now.

But he couldn't leave it. Her attitude to their relationship bothered him. "So what am I to you? Simply a bolthole you make for when your parents get heavy? I get the impression you're not really settling in Oldston."

If things got tough, like they had in the past, Suzy might walk away again. And this bothered him.

"I came here first — remember! You are living in the house I rent! So you've got it wrong. This is where I've made my home. Do I say anything about missing Norfolk?"

"No, but you're not happy, are you? Not really."

"I've got a good job. I'm making friends and Matilda is certainly settled. What more do you want?"

"Matilda is a child. She'd settle anywhere as long as we were with her. You don't seem to be committed to this relationship. I'm looking for more than just a live-in lover," he said.

"Live-in lover . . . I rather like it," she said. "It makes me feel naughty. I quite like having a man in my bed who's not my husband. It'll give me a certain kudos at work. What about you?"

"It unsettles me, that's what it does."

"Then get over it. We're fine. I don't know what else to say to convince you."

"If we did get married, it wouldn't have to be a big affair. Just you, me and a couple of witnesses."

"Not now, Stephen."

Irritation was creeping back into her voice. Greco shook his head. Something was going on, and he'd no idea what it was.

* * *

Screaming and swearing, she stumbled through the club doorway, fell into the gutter and threw up. The bouncer shook his head and went back inside.

"Bastard!" she shouted after him. "My stuff's in there."

Moments later the bouncer reappeared and tossed her bag and a pair of high heels onto the pavement.

She was young. Probably too young to be clubbing. The man watching from the shadows put her at about seventeen. She was skinny with long wavy blonde hair that flowed, dishevelled now, down her back and over her face.

"Having trouble, love? You look cold. That dress doesn't cover much."

"Get lost, perv." She tried to stand but lurched forward onto him.

"Steady on. You've had a skinful by the looks of it. Where are your friends?"

"Dumped 'em. Stupid lot." She pulled a sulky face, brushed her hair back and picked up her bag. "Need a taxi."

"I am a taxi," the man said. He pointed to a car parked a few feet away. "Where d'you want to go?"

She made no reply and staggered round to the back of his car.

"You haven't got one of them plate things," she said. "You could be anyone."

Parents' words. She'd have been told many times never to do this.

"My daughter's about your age," he said. "She's at the sixth form now, doing A levels."

It seemed to reassure her. "I go there," she said, and smiled.

"My Annie broke her wrist or it'd be her I was waiting for," he said. "She loves going to that place." He nodded towards the club. "Cheap drinks and good music, so she tells me. Which way are you going?"

"Towards the Link."

"My fare hasn't turned up. At least let me get you away from this part of town. It's not the place for a young girl to be alone at night. Anything could happen."

"I should ring my mum," she said. She rummaged in her bag.

"Tell her you've got a taxi. Tell her not to worry."

The girl nodded. "You could speak to her."

"No, just tell her you'll be home soon. It's easier."

She swiped buttons on her phone. He listened to the conversation, which quickly turned into an argument. Finally she threw her phone back into her bag.

"Stupid woman just goes on and on about how late it is. Can you believe she's been walking the streets looking for me? I told her I was coming here and I said I'd be late."

"I'll have you home in no time. Come on."

"She asked me to send a photo of your plate," she said, looking again at the rear of the saloon. "What shall I do?"

"It must have fallen off as I came over the bridge. I'll have to get another one made tomorrow."

"I could photograph the registration plate," she said, and took a shot.

"You shouldn't keep your mother waiting. Hop in and let's go."

"I'm trying to send her the picture but I can't see anything back here," she said.

"There's not much signal round here anyway. I'd give it up if I were you." He watched her throw the phone onto the seat beside her.

"Does your daughter like the sixth form?"

"Yes, I think so. It's hard work but she needs the grades for uni. She wants to be a vet," he said.

"I don't know what I want to do. My mum says I should get a job and earn some money. But there isn't anything out there for people my age, is there? My mum doesn't know what she's talking most of the time."

"Even so, you don't want to worry her. You've had a lot to drink. Here, get this down you." He threw her a bottle of water. "It'll sober you up."

He drove round the back streets, avoiding the CCTV on the main roads. He was pleased. It had gone like clockwork, just like the last one.

She was practically lying down on the back seat now. With what he'd put in that water, she'd be out of it soon. He drove slowly, and as he turned into Archibald Terrace he turned off the car headlights.

"Come on, girlie, we're here. Time to have some fun." She was dopey as he helped her out, so she didn't ask questions or struggle. He took the key from his pocket and let them into the house. He chuckled at the confusion on her face as she walked through the door. It changed to a look of terror when she saw what was waiting for her.

Chapter 6

Day Two

At five the next morning, Greco's mobile became a buzzing glow on the bedside table. He grabbed it and looked. The station.

"Who is it at this hour?" Suzy groaned.

"Trouble. Something must have happened," he replied.

"Go downstairs and take it, Stephen, or you'll wake Matilda."

He grabbed his dressing gown and went down.

"Duty sergeant, sir," the voice began. "Archibald Terrace. A woman heard screaming from the empty house next door. She went round the back and saw someone leaving. Whoever it was had left the back door open. She got her husband to go inside and check." There was a few seconds' silence. "From what she said it sounds like the other one, sir. Like the one on Arnold Street."

Greco's stomach churned.

"What is it?" Suzy had come downstairs to join him.

"The case. I need to go. We've got another one."

"What's going on, Stephen? Two murders in as many days?"

She was right to be concerned. Whoever was doing this had been busy. These killings weren't spontaneous. The house, getting hold of the key, it all took organising. But how did he select his victims? Greco had been looking to Jessie Weston's life to provide a clue, but there was no clue. Apart from her rather volatile relationships with those close to her, Jessie had led a normal life.

"Will you come back, have some breakfast and get ready properly?" Suzy asked. "You have a routine in the mornings. If you deviate too much, you'll be uncomfortable all day."

He looked at her, his face grim. "I have to go. I can't do anything else. I'll try and get an hour later on to sort myself out."

"You should eat at the very least. Ring me if you need anything. We're having staff development today, so no students. I can easily get away."

He'd been doing well with Suzy's help. He couldn't lose her again. It would do him no good at all to go through the upheaval of a second break-up. Suzy kept his life simple. Everything was in its place, meals were on time, and the household ran smoothly. If she left him again, he'd crumble. He knew he would.

"I'll be fine," he said. He kissed her cheek and went back upstairs to get dressed.

* * *

By the time Greco got there half the street had been taped off, front and back. Archibald Street was short, with twelve terraced houses either side. The house in question, number four, had a 'for sale' board outside it. Harvey & Son were handling the sale.

"The bloke next door is really cut up," a uniformed officer told him. "His wife was putting rubbish out in the bin when she spotted the intruder. Whoever it was had left the back door open. She got her husband to have a look inside. He wouldn't let her go in. It's really bad in there."

"How far are we from Arnold Street?"

"Top of here, turn right, then it's the second street along. No distance at all."

"Have the people from the Duggan arrived?"

"A local GP confirmed death, not that there could have been any doubt, according to the neighbour. Doctor Barrington and her team arrived five minutes or so before you. They're in there now."

Greco inhaled deeply. He knew the scene inside the house was going to be bad. He heard someone call his name. It was Speedy. He appeared in the doorway, ashen-faced.

"It's awful in there," he said. "It's like a bloody slaughterhouse. The neighbour two doors down has made some tea. I'll get a mug if you don't mind. Want some?"

Greco shook his head. "How old?"

"Young. Teens, I'd say." Speedy's voice quivered as he spoke.

"Everything's very much as yesterday except that there's a lot more blood," Natasha Barrington told him when he went inside. "Stripped naked, strung up from a beam, speared through the heart with something hot. More of that awful cutting to the face and raped. The blood is everywhere, even up the walls. He pierced the aorta and it's splattered everywhere."

"Her name was Rosa Hudson," Roxy Atkins said.

"Have the photos been taken?" Greco asked.

"He's just started."

The photographer briefly pulled the mask from his mouth and smiled.

"You met Mark at Arnold Street," Roxy explained. "Mark Brough, one of our new crime scene investigators. If there's anything you want to know and I'm not available, just ask him."

"Get everything done as quickly as you can and take her down."

Natasha looked at Greco's face and nodded.

"She was very young. Pretty too," Mark said.

"Expert, are you?" Greco said.

"No — but they both were, and blonde. There might be something in that."

"You stick to what you do and leave the detective work to us," Greco snapped.

"Look, this is no easier for us than it is for you," said Mark. "She's young, she's pretty, it's a damn waste. That's all I meant."

"Do we know anything other than her name?"

Roxy Atkins nodded. "We have her provisional driving licence."

"We'll take samples of everything, Stephen. But whoever he is, this guy is good," Natasha said. "The forensic team went over the property in Arnold Street with a fine tooth comb and got nothing."

"But he leaves their ID behind. He makes it easy for us to find the families. Why is that, do you think?"

"Rubbing it in? Wants to cause as much pain as he can? Who knows what goes on in the minds of such people, Stephen?"

"Does anyone know how she got here?"

"The neighbour thinks in a car. A dark coloured one, about midnight," the uniformed officer said. "I've asked along the street, but apart from the screaming no one noticed anything."

"How did he get in?"

"He must have had a key because there's no sign of a break-in."

"Like I said, much as before," Natasha said.

Greco turned on his heel and went back outside. He'd seen enough. The look on the girl's face had chilled him to the bone.

"Sir?" Roxy Atkins called out. "She has a stamp on her wrist from a club in town. Her clothing also suggests that's where she'd been last night."

"Any idea which one?"

"*The Rave* I'd say from the stamp. Her clothing was folded like the last one and a square of fabric is missing from her dress."

So he was taking trophies. She was unlikely to have gone to the club alone. Someone might know who she left with. He went in search of Speedy.

"Who called you?" Greco asked Speedy.

"The station, at some ungodly hour this morning. By the time I got here, uniform had sorted the area and rung the Duggan."

"Any ideas?"

"He's a bloody nutjob. I reckon he stakes out the property first. He seems to use a certain type of house. He likes them old, needing work, and with a fireplace to heat that poker thing he uses." Speedy tossed the remains of his tea into the gutter. "First he works all that out, then he goes on the hunt."

"Very good. My thoughts too. That means this house was already set up prior to last night. It's the getting in that's puzzling me. There's no break-in, so he has to have had a key. I can't believe that no one saw or heard anything. He must have visited at some time before bringing the girl."

"That estate agent needs another visit if you ask me. Slimy sod. He must know something. Both houses are on his books. Bit of a coincidence that."

"Get the team down here and knock on every door. Do Arnold Street again, too. Speak to everyone. Make it a priority."

"These people don't say much, sir. The curtains twitch a lot. I'm sure some of them see more than they'll admit to. But they don't want dragging into any of this."

"Keep at them. Sooner or later one of them will give us something. These girls didn't live in the area. The latest girl would have stood out, all that blonde hair and being so young."

"We've got visitors, sir."

Greco looked at a red car that had pulled up a few yards away.

It was the press.

"Looks like you've got another one, Inspector," a voice called out. "Got anything to say? Fancy giving us that press conference yet?"

"Laycock!" Speedy turned his back on the man. "Bloody pest."

A uniformed officer went to have a word and moments later the reporter drove off.

"What's the betting he'll be back with cash in his hand the minute we've gone," Speedy said. "I bet he gets some response from the greedy buggers on this street."

"It's still very early," Greco said. "How come Laycock got to know so soon?"

"We could always drag him in and ask," Speedy said. "I'd like to see that bastard squirm."

"We might just do that. Are you going back to the station?"

"I'm nipping home first, get some breakfast. I'll be back in about an hour with the team."

Greco nodded. Speedy made for his car. Greco went back into the house. "What else did she have in her bag, apart from the licence?" he asked Roxy.

"Just some make-up and a few coins."

"No phone?"

"No, and that's odd given her age. You know what they're like, these kids."

"Let me take a photo of the licence. I'll visit the address shortly and speak to the parents."

"I don't envy you that one," Natasha said. "You must really hate that part of the job."

Greco nodded. She had no idea how much.

"The PM will be later today, but she'll need identifying officially first. Let me know when you've found her next of kin."

The prospect of having to give some unsuspecting parents the dreadful news turned Greco's stomach.

"Inspector!" It was Roxy Atkins. "There is what looks like the remains of a mobile phone in the fire embers. The plastic bits have melted, but we still might get something."

"He must have thrown it in there. She could have called someone or sent a text. Get onto the service provider for the records, will you?"

Roxy nodded.

Greco decided that he'd go home before going to the station. He doubted that he could eat any breakfast. He wanted to clean up again, and to catch Suzy and Matilda before they left.

* * *

"More mayhem?" Suzy said.

"The very worst. Don't ask. The details are sickening." He whispered this so his daughter wouldn't hear.

"Why couldn't you have gone into teaching, or social work or something, Stephen? I don't think police work is doing you any good."

"It's the choice I made. I can't do anything else." This was an old argument and he didn't want to have it now.

"You're not coping. Your colleagues don't see it, but I do. You need to think about it. Stress is a killer."

He didn't reply. Matilda was in her uniform, ready for school. He picked her up and spun her around. "Got anything exciting on today, Tillyflop?"

"I've got to write a story about Mortimer, then I have to read it out to the class," she told him proudly. "He's been really good and eaten all his breakfast."

"We'll have to leave," Suzy said. "I'll drop Matilda off and get into college early if you're sure you can manage. This staff development is all about a college inspection so I'd better show my face."

"I can take her if it helps," Greco said.

"We have to take Mortimer too," said Matilda.

"He can sit in the back with you."

"Are you sure, Stephen? You look very edgy. Do you need some time before you go back to work?"

"No. It's better if I just get on with things."

"Look, why not shower and change and I'll make some coffee. Half an hour won't hurt. Matilda doesn't have to be there until nine."

There was no way he could hide anything from Suzy. She saw it all. "We are okay, aren't we?" he said.

"Yes. Stop worrying."

"Only, after yesterday I thought perhaps you wanted all this to stop."

"No. I'm fine. But you are not easy to live with, are you? Work comes first, it always has. You can't blame me, Stephen. It was work that got in the way the last time."

"It's what the job is. Crime doesn't do nine to five."

"But you could, if you did something else."

So there it was. She wasn't happy with him staying in the force. So why not just come out and say it? They would have to talk some more — but not now.

By the time Greco returned to the sitting room he was feeling better. Suzy was staring out of the window at a car parked across the road. He had a look. He wasn't sure but it could be the press. What they hoped to gain by following him home he could only guess at.

"If that man in the car is press, this is harassment. Don't speak to him — about anything," he said. "They're a menace, the whole lot of them. All they think about is getting a story they can sell to the nationals. Well, the crimes we're dealing with are certainly big enough."

"You shouldn't jump to conclusions. He could be anyone. This is really getting to you, isn't it?"

"We've got a messy one on our hands," he said. "The press aren't helping. We can't give them too much because it would jeopardise the case when it comes to court. But they never stop. I don't know how they get wind of half the stuff. We're dealing with the locals at the moment — the *Herald* mostly. But the nationals could get hold of it. The case will turn into a circus if they do."

"You need to relax more."

"When this is over. I'll probably be late home tonight," he said.

Her face fell.

"You're not yet forty," she said. "I know you're good at it, but I also know how badly it affects you. I've seen how much you put into the job, how obsessed you get. But you should be enjoying life. It worries me that all you do is work and fret."

"I'm okay. Really," he said. But he could tell from her face that she didn't believe it. "Murdered girls . . . what am I supposed to do? The details are too terrible to tell you. The crime scenes are like something out of a bad horror film. Someone is really going to town, Suzy, and he needs to be caught."

"Okay. I'll keep something hot. Perhaps we can go out at the weekend. I can organise a babysitter. All you have to do is say yes."

"Go ahead. We'll have a meal at that place you like, by the river," he said. "Come on then, Tillyflop. I'll carry Mortimer to the car."

* * *

The Hudsons lived on a leafy avenue in an area between Oldston and Leesworth. As he pulled up, a silver hatchback was about to drive away. Greco got out and waved for the car to stop. The occupant was a woman in her forties.

"Mrs Hudson?"

She nodded. "What is it? You're blocking my way."

"Can I have a word? Inside perhaps? Is there anyone else at home?"

"What is this? Who are you?"

Greco showed her his badge.

"My husband is in, but Rosa is still in bed I'm afraid."

Greco stared at the woman. "Are you sure? Have you looked in on her this morning?"

"Yes, of course I have. I've even been in with a mug of coffee, but she was snoring her head off. Inspector, has she done something? She's not in trouble, is she?"

The dead girl had had Rosa's driving licence with her.

"Is this hers? Are you sure the girl in the photo is your daughter?" He showed her the mobile phone picture he'd taken of the document.

"Yes, that's my Rosa. She's having lessons. Is that what this is about?"

"No. It's not that simple, I'm afraid. I need to speak to her at once."

"Come inside and I'll get her up. Whatever this is, I'm sure she'll have an explanation. She always does."

The house was warm and comfortably furnished. There was a view of Oldston Park through French doors at the back.

"Sit down," Mr Hudson told him. He was sitting on the sofa reading the morning paper. "There's still hot coffee in the pot if you'd like some."

Greco shook his head.

"What's she been up to now? It's not her driving again, is it? She's having lessons, but Rosa doesn't seem to get any better."

He heard someone thumping their way down the stairs.

A teenage girl walked into the room.

"Where did you find it? I told her not to let it out of her sight. She knows how important it is."

Rosa Hudson looked about the same age as the murder victim. She had long fair hair and was swathed in a fleecy dressing gown.

"Okay. I'll fess up," she said to Greco. "I lent it to Jenna yesterday at school. She needed ID to get into the club. She isn't eighteen yet." She wrinkled her face. "I'm not in trouble, am I? For doing that? It's no biggy. Everybody does it."

"Jenna who?"

"Jenna Proctor. Why, what's she done?"

But the girl wasn't paying attention. She walked over to the French doors and waved to someone in the park.

"Charlie's waiting for me. I'd better get ready."

"Do you have Jenna's address?"

"She won't be up yet," Rosa said. "She'll still be wasted from last night."

"I'm sorry to have to tell you this but Jenna is dead," Greco said. "I need to see her parents as quickly as possible."

The girl took hold of her mother's arm. "Did she have an accident? She didn't take something at the club? I'm always warning her about that. You can get hold of anything there. Some of it is lethal. Is that what happened?"

Greco caught the father's eye.

"Tell us what happened. The two of them were close friends," said Mr Hudson.

"Jenna was murdered," Greco said. "Since she had your ID, I take it you weren't with her last night?"

The girl shook her head. "I work part-time and I couldn't get the night off."

"Do you know who she went out with?"

"A whole bunch of them were going to *the Rave* club in town. There will have been loads. You should ask at school, the sixth form." She thought for a moment. "I think Jack was picking her up. He's soft on her."

"Jack who? Does he go to the sixth form too?"

64

"Yes."

"And do you know where he lives?"

"He lives two houses up from Jenna. Their road isn't far from here."

Rosa's dad had already written down the address. "Go back to the main road, then take the second left. The Proctor house is the detached stone one."

Chapter 7

"Grace, you take Archibald Street with Craig and I'll do this one with a couple of PCs," Speedy told Grace.

They were stood on Arnold Street, ready to knock on doors. Speedy groaned. He looked furious.

"Every door, this time. We need to speak to as many of the residents as possible," he said.

"You need to cheer up," Craig said. "No one's going to talk to a face like that. And while I'm at it, you should try to get on better with the boss too."

"Save it, Merrick. Right now I'm too bloody mad. This bastard is running rings around us. I'm only sticking with the job because he needs catching, it's that simple. He's got to get his and quick." Speedy began hammering loudly on the first door. No answer. He banged again.

"How are you doing?" Grace held out a flask to him.

"It's a waste of time. We won't get anything from this lot. When they do answer the bloody door, they wind me up. Questions, that's all I get. They're fishing for info to sell, and sod what's happened to those poor girls. Wait until I see that bloody Laycock. What about you?"

"Nothing that we don't know already. The people who live on Archibald Street are like those monkeys — see nothing, hear nothing and the other one." She smiled. "Coffee? Warm you up."

"What have you done with Craig?"

"Ernest Talbot's bending his ear. He's an old windbag. Just keeps going on about the press and how we should get them on our side."

"I'm going back to the station," Speedy said. "I've had enough."

"You can't do that. Greco will expect some results. What's wrong, Speedy? You're a right misery these days."

"The truth is, I've had it. With this town, with the people in it, but most of all with this bloody job."

"We all get days like that, and this case is a bad one."

"This isn't just one of those days, Grace. I can't do this anymore. I feel like my whole bloody life is going down the pan. I hate the job. I'm sick and tired of how it keeps kicking me in the guts."

"Tell Greco. Tell him how you feel. Tell him why you're not happy with the job."

"If I do that, he'll think I've gone soft."

"No he won't, Speedy. Greco's not like that. He'll try to help. He's a good guy, he'll understand."

"I wouldn't bet on it."

"He does have a different side, Speedy. He's not all 'intense detective,' you know. You should try and see what is beneath the surface. Part of it's his uneasiness with people." She paused. "C'mon, Speedy, you know what he's like. He doesn't do emotions very well. But under all that stiff upper lip stuff is a compassionate family man. I know he will understand."

"I reckon you're talking about a different bloke."

"At least think about it. What harm can it do? Right now you're down and not thinking straight. You've got to speak to someone. Your job's important. There's nothing else for you out there."

"Don't you think I haven't realised that? It scares the hell out of me."

"Come on, I'll help you do this street. It won't take long with the both of us."

"Thanks, Grace. But talk to Greco? I don't fancy that."

"You're the police." A middle-aged man greeted them at the next door. He was drying his thinning hair with a towel. "Disturbed my beauty sleep the other night you lot did. So what d'you want now?"

"There's been a murder in one of these houses," Speedy said, showing his badge. "Did you see or hear anything out of the ordinary?"

The man sighed. "This is a quiet street as a rule, but there's been a lot of coming and going lately. Down there at number eight, that's where you mean, isn't it? The bloke next door told me the news earlier this morning."

Speedy nodded.

"A man in a dark car was there over the weekend. He had ladders and wore dark overalls. I presumed he was giving the place a coat of paint."

"Can you describe him?"

"No more than forty, tall and he wore a hat, a woollen thing that covered his hair. Darkish glasses."

"Did he stay long?"

"At least an afternoon. Sunday, I think it was. He was a noisy bugger, I know that. He had his radio on dead loud the whole time."

"He had a key?"

"He must have done. The thing is, I saw the car again last night. It was turning out of the street and making for the town centre. I work odd hours and he passed me as I was coming home. I remember because he knocked my wing mirror and didn't stop."

"What sort of car was it?"

"A Ford Focus, an older one, dark blue. I know the colour because it left paint scrapings on my car."

"You'll need to give a statement, and our forensic people will take a look at your car. Is that okay?"

The man nodded. One of the uniformed officers followed him into the house.

"That was good information. Now we should speak to the woman witness, the neighbour on Archibald Street," said Grace.

"What are you hoping for?"

"She may be able to confirm what he's just told us."

"I tried earlier but got no reply," said Speedy.

"We'll try again and if we still get nowhere, then we'll come back."

"Everything's dead easy for you, isn't it?"

"No, Speedy, it's not. This job is all about persistence and bloody hard work."

He had no answer to this. "Okay, we'll go back and join Craig. We've covered this street now, anyway," he said.

When they returned, Craig Merrick had managed to raise the woman's husband.

"We've been expecting you," he said. "Neither me nor the wife has gone to work today. No way could I go. I'm still shaking, and I heard there was another one the day before."

"You told an officer that your wife saw someone leave out the back way," said Speedy.

"Yes. I did." A woman appeared in the hallway. "Creeping about, he was. He had on dark clothing and a woollen hat. I didn't see his face, it was too dark."

"Was he tall, short, overweight?" Speedy asked.

"Tallish, although not as tall as Bert here," she said.

"How long has the house been empty?" Grace asked.

"About two months. When the dementia got worse, old Mrs Johnson couldn't cope anymore. She never had kids so she went into the care home."

"The one by the park?"

"Yes, that's the one."

Grace looked at Speedy. The previous occupants of both houses were living in the same care home. Could it be another piece of the puzzle? But how did it fit? Craig had been right. He wasn't invisible, people had seen him. Their descriptions tallied. The problem was, no one had recognised him. So he wasn't from these streets.

* * *

Greco had parked outside the Proctor house. He sat in the car, staring at the stone walls and imposing double door front entrance. There were two cars on the driveway, and both were large and expensive. He sighed. He couldn't put this off any longer. It would be hard, but he had to get it done.

He was halfway up the drive when a woman appeared at the front door.

"Is it about Jenna?"

She was dressed for work in a suit and high heels, and looked to be in her mid-forties.

"The girl's got no thought for anyone but herself. I told her to tell me if she was staying out. I was up and down the road last night looking for her. She has me worried sick when she does this."

"Mrs Proctor?"

She blinked, and backed away from him slightly.

"I'm DI Greco from Oldston CID. Can we talk?"

She gave him a nervous smile and led the way inside.

"My husband has already left for work. She's not got herself locked up or something, has she? I've got a meeting in half an hour. Stupid girl."

"Are you here on your own?"

"Jonathan!" she called.

Seconds later a tall, skinny youth with long hair appeared at the end of the hallway. "It's Jenna. She's been up to her tricks again," she said.

"Mrs Proctor, perhaps you should sit down."

She began to shake. She gazed at Greco, as he tried to formulate his words.

"Tell me. Just tell me. What can she have done to bring *you* here?"

"I'm afraid Jenna has been killed, Mrs Proctor. I'm very sorry."

The youth put an arm around her shoulder and led her down the hall to the lounge. She wailed and clung to him. Greco followed.

Jonathan Proctor helped his mother sit down. He turned to look at Greco. "You're wrong, I know. This is some sick joke. She's getting back at Mum for being such a cow to her last night."

"Jenna has been murdered," Greco said. "We found her body this morning, in a house in Oldston."

"Murdered . . ?" Jenna's mother said. "Why? Why my Jenna?"

"We don't know," said Greco. "Do you know where she went last night?"

"The Rave club in town," Jonathan replied. "She loved the place. So did half her school year. Ask them."

"Oh, I will," Greco said. "When did you last hear from her?"

"We spoke on the phone, late last night," said Mrs Proctor. "It must have been about midnight. She was on her way home — a taxi, she said. We have an arrangement. Whenever she gets a taxi at night she's supposed to text me a photo of the licence plate. But last night she didn't. I waited. I'd already been out looking for her. When she didn't text, I got annoyed. On weekdays she's allowed out until eleven and no later. We had words and Jenna lost her temper. I presumed she'd gone home with one of her friends."

"I'm going to arrange for a female officer to come and look after you," said Greco. "She'll keep you informed of progress. Are you okay with that?"

Her eyes met his. "Murdered? I don't understand. Why my Jenna? What's she ever done to deserve that?"

"She was simply in the wrong place at the wrong time, Mrs Proctor." Greco paused. "Are you up to making a formal identification?"

"Yes." She sat up straight then, and took hold of her son's hand. "You'll come with me, won't you, Jonathan? We can say goodbye."

"I'd also like an up-to-date photo of her, please."

She went over to the window and took one from a frame on the sill. It showed a teenager with blonde hair and a pretty smile. She looked carefree, happy.

Back in his car, Greco rang Grace and told her about the girls and the mix-up over their identity. "Would you pass the information on to the Duggan? Did you get anything?"

"A little. A man, a stranger, was seen on both streets over the weekend. Two witnesses gave the same general description and he drives a Ford Focus. Also the previous occupants of both the houses are now in the Park House care home. There could be something in that."

"Would you ring them? See what they can add — and well done. We'll go through it when all the team are back. I'm making my way into town to visit the Rave club. Would you ask Speedy to join me there? And would you dig out a young man called Jack Howarth? This is his address. Ask him to come in and have a word with us."

* * *

It was mid-morning by now and Oldston was busy. The traffic on the ring road leading into town was building up. As Greco drove, he spotted an advertising hoarding for the current issue of the *Herald*. It read: *'Police Haven't a Clue.'* Perhaps it was time to speak to them.

The Rave was in part of a disused warehouse just outside the town centre. In daylight it looked unprepossessing, a large square hulk of crumbling red brick with a flat roof. No doubt the entrance looked more impressive in darkness. It had multi-coloured lights strung around it. There were neon signs, and gaudy posters along the wall advertised forthcoming gigs.

Greco banged on the doors. There was no response. The place was locked up tight.

"I bet they don't roll in until after lunch. They don't close until the small hours, remember," said Speedy, walking over to join him.

"There must be someone here, even if it's just to clean up from the night before," said Greco.

"I'll try round the back."

Minutes later Speedy opened the doors and let Greco in. "Cleaning woman. She says the boss will be here shortly."

Greco walked into a huge chasm of a room. There were no windows and few seats.

"Where do they drink?"

"The bar is in the far corner. See the tall tables over there? They stand around them. There are booths for people to sit in but you probably have to reserve them," said Speedy.

The booths consisted of heavily worn fake-leather sofas in semi-circles, with metal tables in the centre.

"The kids aren't bothered what the place looks like. They come here to dance and listen to the music. They chat and they drink. No one sits down much. This isn't a pub, sir."

The floor was concrete and sticky with spilt drinks. "This place should be condemned. It's not fit to allow the public in," said Greco, looking at them dubiously.

"Once the lights are down low and the smoke machine gets going, no one notices the difference. You must have been young once?" Speedy smirked. "Don't you remember what it was like?"

Greco shuddered. "I would never have paid good money to come to a dump like this."

"It's only a fiver on the door, but the drinks are top whack."

"Age range?"

"Seventeen to twenty, no older. By the time they reach twenty they've got more sense."

A man came up behind them. He was heavily built and dressed in jeans, T-shirt and a leather jacket. "Joss Taylor. I'm the manager. I also double as a bouncer on week nights."

Greco showed him his badge. "So you were on the door last night?"

The man looked puzzled. "What's going on? The licence and everything is in order. We don't get much trouble in here. There's no drug-taking or dealing, if that's what you're thinking."

Greco let this pass. He showed Taylor the picture of Jenna Proctor. "We're interested in this girl. She was here last night and left early, about eleven thirty or twelve."

Joss Taylor studied the photo for a few seconds. "Yes, I know her. Right little madam. Well, we operate a dress code here, Inspector."

Greco's eyes widened. A dress code? In this dive!

"We like the males to wear shirts, and the girls should be in dresses, not jeans. That sort of thing. We also like the girls to keep their shoes on. This one was always kicking hers off. I asked her nicely, gave her ample warning, but then she started with the abuse. That's one foul-mouthed young lady when she gets going."

"And she got abusive last night, so you threw her out?"

"Had no choice. She was sick too, all over the floor over there. Too much vodka and no food."

"What happened then?"

"She got a taxi, I think. She stumbled about a bit, finally made it to the door, threw up again and then some bloke went to her rescue. I left her to it."

"This bloke. Did you get a look at him?" Speedy asked.

Joss Taylor shrugged. "Didn't take much notice. I was glad to be rid of the stupid cow."

"I suggest you start to think hard about the details, Mr Taylor. Jenna Proctor was found murdered this morning."

Speedy's phone rang and he walked away to take the call.

"I only caught a glimpse. I was more interested in getting her out of here. He was a tall bloke, wearing one of those woolly hats. I thought that was odd because it's quite warm now. The car was dark," he added. "But that's about it. I'm sorry. We were busy, and every hand is needed to run this place."

"Sir, Grace's been on. There's been a development and she thinks we should go back to the station," Speedy interrupted.

The two detectives went outside. Greco looked around but there was no CCTV. "A dark car around midnight? We could check the cameras on the main streets. Archibald Street is on the other side of town."

"What's the betting he avoided them all?" said Speedy.

"It's got to be worth a try though. What's the emergency?"

"Something about a letter," Speedy said.

Chapter 8

"This has forced our hand."

DCI Green waved an envelope at Greco. "I've called a press conference for five. I thought you and DS Quickenden, plus myself."

"He sent that to the press, and nothing to us?"

"Yes, and to Laycock of the *Herald* of all people. This maniac has outlined our shortcomings in glorious detail to that pain in the arse." He handed Greco a copy of the letter. "This is what Laycock received."

The writer called the investigating officers incompetent fools. He said they would never catch him, and that his reign of terror was only just beginning. He also mentioned both girls by name, although the letter gave no details about what had been done to them. He had signed himself *smiley mouth*. Was that a reference to how he'd cut them?

"We can't be sure that these came from the killer," Greco said. "Apart from the girls' names, there are no other details. That signature could mean anything. But why goad us like this? Why would a killer want to draw attention to himself in this way?"

"Who knows? But we have to get him, Stephen. The press are like a pack of wolves and we can't keep this under wraps any longer. What have you got so far? Is anyone even remotely in the frame?" Green asked.

"No, no one. Both victims led very different lives. The only thing they had in common was being in the wrong place at the wrong time. It strikes me that he's more interested in getting the venue right. He chooses the houses very carefully because he needs to prepare. Then, when he's ready, he strikes."

"The houses were similar and both were up for sale. The agent must have some idea, surely? You've checked who viewed them?"

"No one has shown any interest in either house, sir," Greco said.

"And you're sure the agent isn't lying?"

"He has no reason to. Is Laycock here?"

"Yes. He's waiting in a soft interview room down on the ground floor. I don't want him seeing anything up here. Particularly not that." He pointed to the incident board.

"I'd like a word with him first. I don't want him stirring things up with the rest of them, or printing a load of rubbish in his paper. For now, I'd prefer if it was kept quiet," said Greco.

"You can try, but I doubt he'll go for it. He's got a story and he wants the readership and the sales."

"And we've got a job to do. Right now the killer thinks he's calling the shots. Printing this is simply playing into his hands."

* * *

"Mr Laycock? I'm DI Stephen Greco." He sat down facing the reporter.

Greco had only ever seen Laycock from a distance. Up close, he was a tall, well-built man with dark hair cut very short and a stubbly beard. Greco thought women would probably consider him good-looking.

"I've looked at the letter. It's interesting, but there's nothing in it that proves it came from the killer."

"Whether it does or not, what it says is true," said Laycock. "He's running rings round the lot of you." A small smile curled at the edges of his mouth. "Two young women have been murdered and you don't have a clue. You're getting nowhere fast. He isn't going to stop and we all know it. So I have to ask, DI Greco, how many more innocent girls have to die before you lot pull your finger out?"

Greco felt his hackles rise. He'd only just met the man, and already he disliked him. Laycock set his nerves on edge. "Printing that in your paper won't help matters. It will simply make the people in this town fearful."

"Perhaps they need to be. The killer could well be one of them."

"Do you know something?"

"I know you're wasting time." Laycock leant back in his chair. "In that letter he says it's just the beginning. You need to move fast before another lass ends up butchered. Or perhaps you don't care."

"Firstly, that letter could be from anyone. Cases like this attract all sorts of weird phone calls and correspondence, even confessions. Secondly, me and my team do care. We care very much. It's us that have to speak to family members, attend crime scenes and post-mortems. Do you imagine that we enjoy that? We do things in the course of our work that other folk can't even begin to imagine," Greco replied with cold fury in his voice.

"So it's tough." Laycock was dismissive. "But that's the job. If you can't hack it, I suggest you pass it over to someone who can."

Greco was wasting his time here. He reverted to the usual formula. "We are following a number of leads. I cannot discuss with you any progress made to date. You know that. I suggest you attend the press briefing with the others and only print what we give you."

"You'd like that, wouldn't you? He chose me because he must know my reputation. I won't be gagged. I'll print what I damn well want and you can't stop me."

"You're quite right. But first ask yourself what good that would do."

"My readers are hungry for information. They want to know what you're doing. They want to know if the streets of Oldston are safe. I intend to tell them." Laycock got up and left.

DCI Green entered the room. "I heard most of that. You tried, Stephen, but the bastard will print whatever salacious gossip he thinks fit and to hell with the truth. That letter might be scathing about us, but it doesn't give any details about the killings. We should be thankful for that at least."

"Has the original letter gone to the Duggan?"

"Yes. Laycock handed it in — after he'd taken a photocopy of course."

"Sir!" Craig Merrick stuck his head around the door. "We've had the care home on the phone. The nurse got back to us. Grace had asked if anyone had visited the women and if they had keys to the houses. The nurse said she could do with speaking to someone about it."

"I'll see to the press, Stephen," Green said. "You go and speak to her."

* * *

"Both women, Mrs Baxter and Mrs Johnson, came here recently. Neither can cope alone anymore. Then, after I spoke to your officer something occurred to me," Lorraine Hopkirk told Greco. "She was asking if she could speak to the women about access to their old houses, particularly about who would have had a key."

"Are the women able to talk to me?"

"Not really. Doreen Baxter might, but you have to catch her just right. Mostly she tends to ramble."

"So how do you think you can help, Miss Hopkirk?"

"We offer a lot more here than residential care. We have a day centre and we operate a carer service for the local council. Before both women came to live here they had visits several times a day from a carer. To get them up, washed, make sure they had food, that type of thing."

"Does that mean that your staff would have keys?"

"No. The same carer doesn't visit the same patient each day, so all keys are kept in a safe at the house. We fit a small metal box to an outside wall which can only be accessed by a four digit code. That way all of our carers can get in at any time."

"And both the houses had these safes?"

"Yes. Since they were terraced houses the safe would be situated on the wall at the back of the house near to the electricity and gas meters."

No one had mentioned noticing these, but it was worth another look. "A small metal box, you say?"

She nodded. "Of course there may well be other people who had a key but in these cases, I doubt it. Neither women had close relatives and before our involvement they spent most of their time alone."

"I see. How many residents do you have in a similar situation? I'm thinking of someone who has come here recently. Someone who has left an empty house, an old house needing work, and one with a key safe, possibly from that same area."

"We have a few. I'd have to do you a list," she said. "Someone recently arrived? Most of our residents have been here a while and the properties they left behind have been re-let or sold by now. But there is someone. Dora Stevens came to us a week ago. She lived on Pierce Street. That property is on the market and it will need a lot of work."

"So where is the key to her house now?"

"Still in the key safe, I suppose. Eventually the safes are taken down and the keys given back to the landlord or the new owner. In the case of the two ladies you are interested in, this hasn't happened yet. There is no rush, you see. If the properties are rented we wait for the nod from the landlord. Each safe has a telephone number on it and they can ring in when they want it removed."

"Can I have the address of the house on Pierce Street?"

"Number forty-two."

It was worth a look. According to the letter, the killer didn't intend to stop. He would be looking for his next house.

"The man we're looking for could have a connection to this place. He knows the system. If you see or hear anything you think might be relevant, let me know." He handed her a card.

"You think a man who comes here, who visits a relative, perhaps even his mother, could be the killer?"

Greco didn't comment. "Did you have reason to contact Jessie Weston the night before last — ask her to come in?"

"Jessie, yes. Her granny is in here. She was being difficult, becoming overwrought. Jessie had always said she would come, whatever time of day or night it was. She was the only one who could calm the old lady, you see."

This was useful information. Greco knew he should return to the station and find out about the outcome of the press conference, but he didn't have the stomach for it. Instead he decided to have a look around the two properties again, and see if the key safes were still intact.

Looking at a detailed map of the area, he could see that all three streets were very close together. Pierce Street was exactly halfway between the other two. Greco parked his car on Arnold Street and walked to number eight. The street was dark and gloomy. There was only one street light and it was positioned at the far end. It didn't so much illuminate the area as cast weird grey shadows. All the houses looked badly in need of attention, with crumbling brickwork and rotting window frames.

Number eight was locked, with police tape still across the front door. He took a narrow path to the back of the house. There was more police tape across the back gate but it was rickety and loose.

The backyard was small. He crossed old square flagstones with deep cracks between each one. He avoided stepping on the cracks. In one corner was a small shed. Perhaps it had once been an outside toilet. These houses were old. According to an engraved stone at the front, they were built in the 1890s. He could imagine how difficult it would be for an elderly woman to manage a property like this. Keeping it warm would be a losing battle for a start.

There was a small amount of light coming from the kitchen window next door, but it wasn't much help. As his eyes became accustomed to the dark, Greco could see two meters. Both were at one end of the wall next to the fence separating this house from its neighbour. To the left of these was a foot square imprint on the wall, and small holes where something had been removed. The key safe!

Greco took his mobile from his jacket pocket and rang the station. Speedy answered.

"I've found something at Arnold Street. I want forensics down here to take a look and a uniformed officer to keep an eye out." He told Speedy about the keys. "I'm going to check Archibald Street next. It is possible that a house on Pierce Street will be set up for the next one. I'm going to check on it before I call it a day. The nurse at the care home has a new resident from there, and her old house fits the profile. I could be way off beam but it's worth a look."

Archibald Street was exactly the same. The key safe was missing, somehow removed from the outside wall at the back. Greco rang it in and moved on.

Greco walked the few hundred yards to the next house. He went over his conversation with Suzy. He had expected her to jump at the chance of remarrying, but she hadn't. Why was she holding back? After all, it had been Suzy who wanted to restart the relationship. So what was going on? Why had she said she wanted him if she couldn't commit? He would have to talk to her again, try and understand what was going on in her head.

Pierce Street wasn't as claustrophobic as the others. The houses were a little bigger and they had small front gardens. The street was wider too, with parking bays marked on the road. Number forty-two had a 'sold' sign above it. Harvey & Son were the agents again. Greco walked to the top of the street and made his way down the back way between Pierce Street and the houses in the neighbouring road. The house number was painted in gleaming white on the back gate. Someone had already started the refurb. The gate was bolted from the inside. Feeling over the top edge, Greco slid the bolt open and went in.

"There's no one there!" A woman's voice called out. "And there's nothing to steal either. The place has been cleared."

It was the next door neighbour.

"I'm the police!" he called back. "I'm just checking the yard. Has there been anyone else here recently?"

He heard her laugh. "Hundreds."

"Prospective buyers?"

"And workmen. Bloody nuisance with their noise. One of them had his radio blaring at midnight. I had to bang on the wall."

"Are they local, the workmen?"

"No idea, love. Don't pay much attention. Mostly it's the white van brigade."

"Thanks."

Greco looked around the yard. He couldn't see any meters but there was a small metal box fixed under the kitchen window. It was labelled with an address for social services and a phone number. The key safe. So if this house was the next target, the killer hadn't finished his preparations.

Chapter 9

Day Three

"She swore at me."

"Is that why you made such a flaming mess?"

"Her language was bad. I had to make her stop. I did things right — what the voices told me to." It was alright, though. *He* was pleased. *He* was grinning back.

"Glad it wasn't my place you trashed."

"I couldn't help it. I did what the voices said. I did everything right. The mess wasn't down to me. It was her."

"It's okay, Neville. Just calm down."

"Can I do another one? I'm getting the hang of it now. It's fun."

"We'll see. Depends what the voices say."

"I hear them." Neville tapped his head. "They don't leave me alone. They want me to do another one. You should hear what they say."

"Take your pills, Neville." *He* handed him a bottle.

They were small and white and they made Neville sleep. The other ones, the ones from the doctor, had made the voices go away. These made them louder. But that didn't matter, because the voices were his friends now.

"I know who I want next. I've seen her."

"It doesn't work like that, Neville."

"I keep thinking about it. I want to go out."

"No. You'll get into trouble on your own. You stay here and don't answer the door. I'll be back after work."

"Will the police come?"

"No, Neville. They don't know it's you. They don't know who it was. And we'll keep it that way."

"Can I tell them? I won't be 'Naff Neville' then, will I?"

"No. You'll be *mad Neville* and they'll lock you up."

"I've got to go to Springbank today."

"You don't need that place."

"Mrs Rowcroft — Edna — says I do. She thinks going there is doing me good." He missed Edna. She was nice. She was a big, comfortable woman and she smiled a lot. She smiled at Neville, and no one else did. "No matter how much I swear or carry on, she doesn't shout at me. She's on my side."

"It's an act. That's what she wants you to think. *I'm* on your side, Neville, and I'm the only one who is. Understood?"

"She'll go on at me if I don't go."

"I don't want you wandering around. Like I said, you'll get into bother."

"I won't."

He was losing it. Neville winced as *he* slammed a mug down on the table. He'd gone too far.

"Do as you're told. Stay put and give us both a break."

* * *

They were all in by eight the next morning, even Speedy. Tension was high. They wanted to catch the killer. Greco told the team about the key safes and set about updating the incident board. The words 'loud music' caught his eye.

"A woman on Pierce Street said the bloke she thought was a workman played his radio loud. It got on her nerves," he said.

"The man in the dark overalls wearing a woollen hat," Grace added. "We were told about him too. He spent time at the house on Archibald Street. Same man?"

Greco circled the word 'radio.'

"Are you okay, sir? You look tired."

Someone was bound to notice. He hadn't slept a wink. There was too much on his mind: the case, as well as Suzy and where their relationship was going. He felt untidy, dishevelled, and it made him uncomfortable. He still needed to get his hair cut and he'd had no time to iron the shirt he'd taken from the wardrobe. Despite insisting she ironed all his stuff carefully, Suzy wasn't careful enough.

"Lot to think about." He tried to smile.

"We'll get there, sir. We usually do."

"Yes, but I'd like to get there before another young girl loses her life," he said. "This man, Grace, do we have a description?"

"Tallish. Dark glasses, dark overalls, wearing a woollen hat. Everyone who saw him presumed he was working on the houses."

"He hasn't come forward. He could be our man," said Greco.

"The sighting at Archibald Street was him preparing the next one. We need to check with the agent. No one was taking much notice until he annoyed them with his music," said Grace.

She was right.

"A mistake? Or was he drawing attention to himself?" Greco said.

It was a mystery. Greco had no idea why he'd do such a thing. The office phone rang. It was Roxy Atkins from the Duggan.

"Inspector Greco, we had a look at all three properties last night. "I found a blood smear on the wall at Archibald Street where the safe was. Only a little, as if someone had scratched themselves removing the box. But it's enough. I'll run a DNA profile and check it against Jenna Proctor. If it isn't hers, then it has to belong to whoever removed that safe. Apart from that, nothing else yet."

"Thanks. I'll pass it on to the team. Keep us posted."

He turned to the team. "He's possibly made his second mistake. Blood has been found on the wall at Archibald Street," he said.

"What are we doing about Pierce Street?" DC Craig Merrick asked. "Do you want someone to camp out there?"

"No. They'd be noticed. Forensics has agreed to put up surveillance cameras, small ones in the sitting room and on the back wall. They can be accessed remotely over the internet. If our man shows, then we'll know."

"How will they get the keys?" Grace asked.

"We'll do that this morning. Speedy and I will go back and speak to Harvey & Sons. You and Craig do some more digging. Go back and speak to Megan Hunter and Frankie Farr. Ask Frankie about the relationship, and where it was going. Megan Hunter didn't mention the arguments, so ask her about them. Also this young man, Jack Howarth." He handed Grace the address. "He was Jenna's boyfriend and would have been at the Rave with her. See what he says. Ask how the evening went. It will do no harm to talk to the people at the Rave again. Keep them on their toes." He paused for a moment. "Laycock bothers me. Someone told Mavis Weston what happened to Jessie. Was it him? If so, why would he do that?"

"Do we bring him in?"

"Not yet."

"This lad, Jack Howarth. Does he go to the sixth form?"

"Yes. You'll probably find him there. Speak to him and Jenna's other friends. Find out what they remember about that night."

"Have you seen the papers, sir?" Speedy asked.

"No, and I missed the conference. Did Laycock give you much trouble?"

"No, he was surprisingly quiet. But look what the bastard printed today."

Greco took the tabloid Speedy handed him. They were front page news — the police, that is, not the murders.

"Trouble is, people will believe it." Grace shook her head.

"We could do with a result, something to take the heat off," Speedy added.

"We're doing our best. Once forensics has done their bit, we should be in with a chance. At the moment they're looking at paint scrapings from the car, what's left of Jenna's mobile and now the blood trace. Any one of those could give us a lead."

* * *

Neville wanted to go out. It couldn't do any harm, surely? The man who gave him the pills went out all the time. No one tried to stop him. He had to do something. The voices were driving him mad and his head was aching. Neville needed to do something to kill the voices. Anyway, Edna was waiting for him at Springbank. She'd give him tea and cake. She'd make him feel special and he liked that. She made him feel as if he mattered.

Sod it. He'd go. He just wouldn't tell.

The noise in town was good. It stopped the voices for a while. It was the same with loud music. The radio on full blast was just perfect. Blotted out everything.

But there were too many people. Neville didn't like crowds. He kept his head down and pulled his coat collar up around his ears. He didn't want anyone to recognise him. He'd have to talk to them then. *He'd* said that he had to keep his nose clean or there'd be trouble. It was alright for him. *He* had a life. All Neville had were the voices and the memory of what he'd done.

"Hey, Neville! Naff Neville!"

He knew that voice. Bloody hell, now he'd get dragged into something and *he* wouldn't like it.

"Hold up, man, where you off?"

"Nowhere." He didn't stop walking. He didn't even look up. Neville didn't like Dan Roper. He'd met him at Springbank. Edna hadn't liked him either. She'd said he was a bully.

"Liar. You've got something on. Come on, Naff. Tell Dan what's going down."

He hated that name: Naff Neville. It'd been his nickname ever since school. Who calls their kid *Neville*, for fuck's sake!

"Springbank House."

What was the use? If he didn't tell the bastard, the name calling would begin in earnest. And that would make him mad.

"That place's for losers." Dan sniggered. "Fancy one of these instead?"

He held out a small plastic bag of what looked like smarties. "I won't charge. Come and have some fun."

"I know what they are. They're dangerous. I'm clean now, given it up."

"Don't give me that. You'll never be clean. You're an addict. Nothing but a sad little druggie."

He was sneering. Neville didn't like that. Dan wanted to get him high on those pills and make him do things.

"Come on, let's give those kids in the park some grief."

Dan whacked him on the back of the head.

"Can't. You should leave me alone."

Dan laughed. "Why, Naff? You dangerous all of a sudden?"

If only he knew. Neville tried to smile. He was seriously tempted to tell him the truth. That would shut him up. But if he did that, he'd have to do him to keep him quiet.

"You can spare half an hour," Dan insisted. "I've got pills and beer. Look." He produced two cans from his coat pocket.

"I fancy a beer, but I'm not allowed to drink."

"You're not a kid. You've a mind of your own. C'mon. Down by the skating rink?"

"Yeah. Alright." The beer had swung it.

They made their way through the park gates, past the play equipment and onto the rink. No longer for roller skaters, it had been converted for skateboards. It was all stainless steel and ramps. Neville stared at it, his mouth open. Why did things have to change all the time?

"Good, aren't they?" Dan handed him a can while they watched the young boarders do their stuff.

"Fancy a go?"

Stupid question. Neville shook his head and took a hefty swig from the can.

"Go on. Show 'em what you can do. I dare you. Get it right, and I'll give you some of these." He waved the pills.

He was taking the piss again. Things never changed.

"I've got to go."

"We've only just got here."

Dan shook the bag of pills in front of his face again. "Cheer you up a bit."

"What are they?" Neville eyed the pink pills with suspicion. They could be anything. No way was he going to risk it.

"Legal highs. You need to chill, mate."

"I'm off." He stood up and lobbed the half-full beer can at the kids on the rink. They hurled a torrent of abuse at him as he walked away. Neville covered his ears. He didn't want to hear. Dan followed. He leapt about behind Neville, shouting, calling him names, teasing him.

Neville was angry. It always ended this way. He'd been the target of all the morons in town for long enough. These people understood only two things — fear and power. Trouble was, no one was scared of Neville. Well it was time to show them he could fight back. It was time Dan learned who was in charge. Neville fingered the knife in his coat pocket. Why had he brought it? He smiled. The voices had told him to. They'd said it would make him feel better, and they were right.

Dan was on a roll. He was right at Neville's back, yelling and swearing. If Neville didn't do something he'd follow him right up to the doors of Springbank. He'd frighten Edna. Neville had to make him stop. They'd reached a copse of trees at the far end of the park. Neville was out of breath now and had to stop. But he'd worked it out. He knew what he had to do. The voices were back. They were on his side, egging him on to sort Dan for good. He'd spoil his afternoon with Edna and Neville couldn't have that.

Neville looked around. There was no one about. He turned slowly. One lunge and it was all over. The noise stopped. The look on Dan's face was priceless.

* * *

"I need to understand how your business works, Mr Harvey." Greco sat in the estate agent's office. "Who does the valuations? Who has access? Who shows any interested parties around?"

They were simple enough questions, surely? So why the blank look? The property business was hardly the secret service. "You sell houses, Mr Harvey. Just tell me how you go about it."

"Well . . . it varies." Harvey was looking horrified. "These murders, surely you don't think one of my staff is involved? We're a tight team. I've known them all for years. Mrs Hardy on the front desk, for example, she's been with me for over two decades."

So that was it. The man thought Greco was going to point the finger at one of them. "I'm not making any assumptions. Just describe to me how everything works. I want to be able to rule you and your staff out."

That seemed to calm him down. "The valuations are done by me, and I take the photos for publicity purposes. Occasionally I might need to hire the expertise of an outside firm. If I needed a surveyor, for example, then it'd be Brogans from the office next door."

"And showing potential buyers around?"

"If the seller is still in residence they will do it. If not, then me."

"You've recently sold a house on Pierce Street. Talk me through that one."

"It was owned by an elderly woman, a Mrs Stevens. She'd reached the stage where she couldn't cope on her own anymore. The family are keen for a quick sale. They want the money to pay the care home fees."

"Who have you shown around the house?"

"One couple, that's all. The properties on Pierce Street are in bad shape. Anyone who buys knows they'll have to put their hand in their pocket to bring it up to standard." He consulted his computer. "A Mr and Mrs Hope are buying. In fact the sale is almost completed."

"Doris Hope?"

"Yes, and her husband. They plan to do it up and let it."

"I know Mrs Hope," Greco said. He looked at Speedy. "She used to do a little cleaning for me when I had the flat. She told me about the house only this week." He looked back at Andrew Harvey. "I'll need to take the keys for a while."

"I'm not sure . . ."

"Speak to the family of the seller and I'll speak to Mrs Hope. This is a murder investigation. I'm sure they won't mind. It shouldn't be for long."

Andrew Harvey shook his head and reluctantly handed over the keys. "You're going to look inside?"

"We won't make a mess. Once we've done what we have to you'll never know we were even there," he said.

"Has someone got a grudge against my firm?"

"I doubt it, Mr Harvey. The person we're interested in requires old houses, preferably with a fireplace that is still capable of having an open fire. You deal mostly with that type of house. It's as simple as that."

They left the estate agent still shaking his head.

"Where to now, sir?"

"We've got the keys. We'd better go round to Percival Street and hand them over."

* * *

It was a short drive, no more than five minutes. The street was busy. Greco saw the van from the Duggan parked outside number forty-two. Mark Brough stood beside it.

This was the first time Greco had seen the man when he wasn't shrouded in a white coverall. He was tall and muscular with short dark hair. Greco put him in his early forties. He seemed friendly enough, and eager to help. They went inside together.

"I think three should do it," Mark said. "One on the side wall angled at the key safe, another in the kitchen and one in the sitting room. If he comes here, we are bound to get a reasonable image."

"And we can view the image from the station, on our computers?" Speedy asked.

"Yes. I've set up a user account in the inspector's name. Here are the log-in details. The footage will be stored. You can view it any time. If a camera is activated, all three will send an alert in the form of an email to whoever you choose."

Greco was impressed. "We'll make that Georgina. She spends more time at her computer than we do. Thanks." He smiled.

"All part of the job."

They left the house.

"Got another one, Inspector?"

"What are you doing here, Laycock?"

"I heard a rumour. Word has it that this will be his next venue. That right, Greco?"

"What word? Who told you?"

They'd only just found out about this house themselves, so how had Laycock got the information so quickly?

"What will you do? Leave someone on guard?" Laycock smirked.

"We're a little more sophisticated than that," Greco said.

"Ah, a camera. I get it. Am I allowed to write about this?"

Greco turned to Laycock. "Write about this . . . in fact so much as mention what you think you know to anyone, and I'll have you for obstruction. Do you understand?"

"My lips are sealed, Inspector," he said. He was still smiling.

Chapter 10

The two detectives took half an hour to grab a bite to eat and a coffee at a café in town. Suzy had told him about it. She had recommended it as very clean.

Greco was just finishing a beef sandwich when he got the call.

"A body has been found in Oldston Park. A young man," DCI Green said. "Stabbed. A woman called it in. She'd been playing with her kids and they stumbled over him. The Duggan are on it."

"We'll get down there, sir. Do we know when it happened?"

"Within the last hour, according to Dr Barrington. That part of the park has been sealed off and we are appealing for witnesses."

Just what he needed. It was different from the murders of the girls. For starters, this one didn't sound as if it'd been planned.

"Trouble?" Speedy asked. He was chatting on his phone to Grace.

"A body in the park. Happened within the past hour."

"Did you get that, Grace?"

"Where are they?" Greco asked.

Speedy handed Greco his phone.

"We're outside the Crown, sir. We're about to go in and talk to Megan. Do you want us at the park instead?"

"No, you carry on. Speak to Megan and Frankie Farr, then ring me."

There were uniformed officers at the three park entrances. The copse where the body had been found was taped off.

"Oldston's getting its fair share of aggro these days, Stephen," Natasha Barrington said.

"Aggro we could do without."

"On first look he's been stabbed once in the chest. I'll know for sure when I get him back, but I'd say the blade pierced the heart."

"Nasty." Speedy looked away.

"He's young. Any ID on him?" Greco asked.

"A doctor's appointment card, for earlier this morning. His name is Dan Roper, and I found these in his coat pocket." She held out the packet of pink pills. "We'll run tests but they look like legal highs to me. Might even be homemade."

"If that's the case they could be the reason he was attacked. Things got out of hand. You can guess the rest," Speedy said.

"Anyone volunteered any information?"

"No, Inspector," said Roxy Atkins.

"Have a look around," Greco told Speedy. "Speak to a few of the older kids. See if he tried to sell them any."

"Look at this!" Natasha Barrington parted the hair. "There's a bloody square of scalp missing— about an inch. You know, like with the girls." She examined his clothing. "A square of fabric is gone from his T-shirt."

"What can this possibly have to do with the girls?" Greco said.

"It's connected somehow. The trophy-taking is the same, and that's too much of a coincidence," Roxy said.

"We'll keep the scene contained until the photos have been taken. I'll let you know what we find."

"Mark Brough not on this one?" Greco said.

"No. He drew the short straw last night. It was him that that went out to the houses you rang in," Natasha told him. "I don't know how you lot manage, but we need our sleep, Stephen." She smiled at him.

* * *

Speedy walked through the park. The good weather had brought folk out. People had seen the police and were starting to get curious about what had happened. How long before the press put in an appearance?

A group of young teenagers were hanging out by the skateboard rink, talking to a uniformed officer. Speedy stopped to watch. They were good.

"Anyone bothered you lads this afternoon?" he shouted to the group. "Anything odd? Arguments, fighting, anything like that?"

They whispered amongst themselves for a few seconds. Then one of them spoke up. "He's just asked that." He nodded at the uniform.

Then a tall blonde lad boarded towards him. "Some low life threw a can into the rink. He sat on that bench with his mate for a few minutes. He chucked a can of beer our way then made off. His mate chased after him."

"Did you recognise him?"

The lad shook his head.

"Did he offer you anything? Pills for example?"

Another emphatic shake.

"This can he threw, what happened to it?"

"Doug put it in the bin over there. We couldn't leave it on the rink."

"Which way did they go?"

"Towards the far entrance, through the wooded part of the park."

Speedy donned a pair of nitrile gloves and made for the bin. After spending several minutes up to his elbows in the detritus, he found the can. He went back to the crime scene.

"Seems he drank from this, then threw at some kids on the skateboarding rink," he told Roxy. "It should have his prints on it, even DNA."

"Well done," she said.

Greco was pacing back and forth beyond the taped area, with his head down. Thinking? Speedy couldn't tell. The link with the girls was puzzling, but with a bit of luck they had something — prints. Greco should look a lot happier than he did. So what was his problem?

* * *

Without saying a word, Greco took off. He walked down the shingle path towards the boating lake and ducked behind a group of trees. He'd thought it was her, and it was. She was a couple of hundred yards ahead — laughing. He didn't understand. She should be at work. He checked his watch. It was lunchtime. Perhaps the bloke with her was a colleague? It was a nice day. Perhaps they were simply having lunch in the park, getting some fresh air before the afternoon grind. But Greco knew that wasn't it. Moments later his suspicions were confirmed. The man was kissing her. In that instant his world slipped out of control.

Suzy was having an affair.

He couldn't move. He couldn't feel his feet on the ground. He was having a panic attack. He strained to see, but the man's back was to him and there were too many people in the way. He couldn't stay here. They mustn't see him. He had to move. Taking his phone from his pocket, Greco took a photo of the two of them embracing. Later, when he confronted her, she would be forced to tell him the truth. Tell him who the man was. He needed to hear the truth from her. He turned and walked away.

"Found something, sir?" Speedy asked.

Greco shook his head.

"You've gone a funny colour, Stephen," said Natasha Barrington. "You okay?"

He nodded. What he had just witnessed had robbed him of speech.

"Photos are done," she said.

The body was put into a vehicle and the team from the Duggan got ready to leave. "I'll do the PM mid-morning tomorrow. We could do with confirming identity. Good call that, your sergeant finding the can."

Greco had no idea what she was talking about.

"By the way, Inspector. I've emailed you what I could get from Jenna's phone," Roxy shouted before she drove off.

"Might give us something," Speedy said, coming up behind him. "Where to now?"

"We need to find out where he lived, that, that . . ."

"Dan Roper, sir," Speedy said.

"Yes. Him. His family needs to be told."

Greco stared into the distance. If Suzy left him again, he'd go to pieces. He'd only just kept it together the last time.

"The surgery?" Speedy said. "The doctor's appointment."

"Yes, yes of course — good idea."

The GP practice was only minutes from the park. They walked in silence. Greco hardly knew what he was doing. He was trying to work it out — and failing. Was this man the reason she was reluctant to get married again? He should have realised what was wrong.

When they arrived in the reception area he couldn't even recall what had brought them here.

They were shown into a small waiting room. The nurse pulled a face when she heard Dan's name. "I'll check with Doctor Ali. I don't want to say anything out of turn."

"That means there's plenty to be said." Speedy grinned. "He was carrying drugs so he had a problem. They'll be glad to be rid of him, more than likely."

"The lad's dead, Sergeant," Greco said, finding his voice at last. "He was a victim, stabbed to death in broad daylight. Have some pity."

The doctor entered the room. "Dan Roper. A local troublemaker. He's been in here this morning, all noise and demands. What's he done now?"

"He's been stabbed. Killed," Greco said. "In the park, just a few hundred yards away."

"Have you got the assailant?"

"No. We need some details about Dan. We only have his name at the moment."

"We need his address and next of kin. Anything and everything you can give us," Speedy said.

Greco stared at him. He should have asked that. But all he could think about was Suzy with that man's arms wrapped around her.

"He was in here asking for drugs. Ordinarily I wouldn't talk about my patients, but Roper wasn't ill. He said he was in pain from his joints. But that was a lie. He wanted me to prescribe something morphine-based. I refused, of course. I was certain there wasn't anything wrong with him. He was young, healthy, but an addict."

"Hard drugs?" Speedy asked.

"I'm not sure. He attended a rehabilitation centre some time ago. Did well too, he was clean for a while. But I think he slipped. He'd seemed very fond of strong painkillers lately, and I suspect he was getting the hard stuff off the streets." He handed over a card with Dan Roper's details on it.

"Shall I go, sir? Find someone and get them to the Duggan?"

Greco ignored the question, he was lost in his own world.

"Perhaps you should go back to the station, sir, or even go home. You don't look well."

No he wasn't well. His world had just imploded. He couldn't think. And he was trying to cover up the fact that he was shaking. He couldn't discuss it. It was too personal a matter. If he tried to describe what he'd just seen the words would stick in his throat.

"You could be right." His voice was a whisper. "I'll return to the station. Do a bit there. You get on with this." He tapped the card.

* * *

As soon as he was back in his car, Speedy got on the phone to Grace. "The boss has suddenly gone all weird on me. Happened just like that. We were called to the body in the park, he ducked off for a few minutes and when he got back he'd gone all spaced out and pale."

"Not like him. Had something happened?"

"Not that I could tell."

"Something's gone on. You should pay more attention, Speedy. Did he see someone he knew?"

"I don't know who he knows. The man's a loner. As far as I'm aware he doesn't know anyone."

"That's not true. If he got upset suddenly, then something happened. Did he get a phone call?"

"No. He just walked off."

"I'll speak to him later. He might tell me," she said. "We're on our way to see Frankie Farr again, then we'll be going back in."

"I'm off to the Link — again. As if I haven't seen enough of that place."

"Just get on with it, Speedy. If the boss isn't up to it then you'll have to take up the slack. It's an opportunity to show what you're made of."

Like anyone would notice.

Dan Roper lived in a block of maisonettes at the far end of the Link estate. Speedy knocked on the door and a girl answered.

"DS Quickenden from Oldston CID." He smiled at her.

She was slouching against the half-open door, chewing gum. She was young, probably under twenty, and thin. Her long black hair was bunched on top of her head with tendrils hanging down over her shoulders. Not bad-looking really, if she was done up right.

"Get lost. He's not here." She tried to shut the door. Speedy shoved his foot in the door.

"Do you mean Dan?"

"What if I do?"

"Is this where he usually lives, here with you?"

"So what? We pay the rent."

"Dan has been attacked," he said. "He's been stabbed. Fatally stabbed."

"Dead, is he?" The expression on her face didn't change. "So what do you want with me? I didn't do it. I was 'ere."

"I'm looking for someone to identify the body and tell me about Dan. Who he hung around with, did he have any enemies, that kind of thing."

"You're not dragging me down to no mortuary. I'm not looking at no dead body either."

"But you did know Dan well?"

She shrugged. "Might have."

"Was he afraid of anyone? Had anyone threatened him? We know he dealt drugs."

"Only soft stuff — legal highs and some blow. He hasn't been near the hard stuff in months."

"So why would someone want to kill him?"

"I dunno. He gets on folk's nerves. He winds people up. Can't help himself."

"Where can I find Dan's parents?"

She laughed.

"He never even knew his dad, and his mother did a runner years ago. He's an only one. She left him with his gran but she's dead now."

"So there's no one."

"That's what I said." She spat out the gum and lit a cigarette. "You finished now? I've got stuff to do."

Speedy decided he'd ask the GP to do the identification.

He checked his watch. Grace would be back at the station by now. He'd go back, have something to eat and work out what they'd got.

* * *

"Where's Greco?" Speedy asked Craig. He was back in the main office.

"Not here. I think he went off somewhere. He looked shattered."

"What did you find out about the dead lad?" Grace came in, carrying a pile of paperwork.

"No parents, a bit of dealing, nothing much. Can you check if he has a record?" he asked George.

"We spoke to the landlady of the Crown. She admitted that her relationship with Jessie was often heated. They argued about her hours. She wanted time off to be with Frankie, and Megan wanted her at the pub. So they rowed a lot."

"What did Frankie Farr say?"

"Not a lot, but I don't think he's hiding anything. He's too cut up about it. I'd say it has only just hit him."

* * *

Greco went home. He couldn't face his colleagues at the station, but he didn't feel like facing Suzy either. He had no idea what to say to her. If he asked her outright and she told him there was someone else, he'd be devastated. But if he didn't . . . It'd drive him insane.

He'd thought they were happy. These last months, he'd felt secure in the cocoon of family life. But her lack of interest in getting remarried had set off a warning light in his head. He'd considered a lot of reasons to explain that, but not another man. He sat in an armchair, looking out over the back garden. It looked lovely in the early summer. Suzy and Matilda had planted out a wide flower border that ran along its length. They'd been busy, and the plot was well-tended. There was even a large bunch of flowers from it on the dining table. This was Suzy's house. She'd taken out the lease on it before he moved in, and it was full of her touches. He suddenly felt like a lodger.

"You're early for once." She burst into the sitting room, her arms full of shopping. "You can pick up Matilda from school if you want." She looked at the clock on the wall. "About half an hour."

"I'll have to go back to the station," he lied. "I'm here taking some time out, that's all."

"Whatever, Stephen. Nothing changes with you, does it?" She took the groceries into the kitchen.

Was that it? Was he the problem? Was this down to his odd behaviour and the job? He had to tackle this now. If he didn't, it would eat him up. "Suzy . . ." He followed her into the kitchen. "You've finished early."

"Told you, staff development day. We've all had an early dart. Makes a change." She was smiling.

"You would tell me if things weren't right?"

She turned and stared at him. "What are you getting at? In what way *not right*?"

He looked at the floor. "I'm talking about us. Are we alright?"

"What's brought this on? I'm busy, you're busy. For goodness sake, Stephen, I thought we'd done with this."

"You're different."

"No. I'm exactly the same." She began putting the groceries away.

"Have you got another . . ?" He couldn't say the words. He shook his head and turned away, terrified of her reply.

"Another what, Stephen? Spit it out or leave it be."

"I saw you today, in the park . . ." He stopped and returned to the sitting room. Several minutes passed before she joined him.

"So you know. That's what this is all about." Her voice was flat.

"I saw you kissing another man. That's what it's *all about*."

He watched her. She seemed to be wrestling with her conscience, looking for a gentle way to let him down.

"He makes me laugh," she said finally. "He's fun. But more importantly, he's around. I don't know if it's going anywhere. For now I'm just enjoying the attention. But I won't lie. I like him."

"Who is he?"

"Who he is isn't important."

"And us?"

"We're not married anymore, Stephen. I'm a free agent, and so are you."

She was trying to make it sound like it was no big deal. It wasn't working. He knew Suzy. He could hear the guilt in her voice. "A free agent? What does that mean, Suzy? And where does it leave Matilda?"

"I won't shut you out. She needs you. I want us all to get on. I want you in our lives — when you've got the time."

"Why won't you tell me who he is?"

"Because you'll do something stupid," she said.

She wanted the best of both worlds.

"Do you want me to leave?"

"Not really. Matilda likes you being here. If you move out the upheaval will upset her. It won't do you any good either."

"I'll move into the spare room," he said. "We won't say anything to Matilda just yet."

"I'm happy with that," Suzy said. "Your mobile is ringing."

She went back to the kitchen.

The call was from Grace. "Sir, the camera at Pierce Street — we've got something."

Chapter 11

"It's very dark. Is there anything that can be done to make the images clearer?"

"We'll try, sir. But he's been careful. It's as if he was expecting to be disturbed or spotted. He's wearing the same dark overalls, the hat pulled low over his face and dark glasses. He's trying to come across as a workman."

"He doesn't look at any of the cameras either," said Greco.

"He can't know they are there. They're all well-hidden."

"At least it confirms that Pierce Street is the next house. He must have got the key from the safe outside. Get forensics to take a look."

"Are you feeling better, sir? Speedy said you weren't feeling well."

"Something and nothing, Grace. A bad head. I took a couple of pain killers and I'm fine now," he lied. "What time was that?" He nodded at the images on the screen.

"About half an hour ago, sir. Want to take a look?"

Greco nodded.

Grace drove. Greco didn't speak much. His head felt like it was full of cotton wool.

"Pity about the camera outside, sir," Grace said as they turned into Pierce Street.

"What happened?"

"It failed. We got nothing."

That about summed up the luck they were having on this case. "Those safes are pretty robust. To break them open would require a power tool, and that would be noisy. I reckon the whole thing was removed from the wall and taken away. I was there last night, fairly early on. So he must have taken it later, or this morning."

"Let's hope someone saw him this time."

"Folk around here don't though, do they?" Greco said.

He was right. The next-door neighbours had heard nothing. One reported that her dog had been a bit agitated at about ten the night before. He'd been whining at the door.

Forensics was going over the property. Roxy Atkins was in charge. "There's a pretty clear footprint on the kitchen floor," she told them. "There are some stone flags missing in the backyard. It's been raining and there are several muddy puddles. He was wearing heavy-soled boots and he has big feet."

"That's something." Grace smiled.

"It's all we've got," Greco said.

"There is the blood smear too, Inspector," Roxy said. "The DNA profile on that should be back today."

"Let's hope we find a match. If we don't, he can leave behind all the blood he wants, because we're no closer."

Greco stood in the empty sitting room. The killer had been here. He'd stood in this very room, planning for his next kill. Had he seen the cameras? Greco couldn't get rid of the notion that he was taunting them.

"Sir, Craig's been on. A man who was at the Rave has asked to see us. He knew Jenna and he took some video snippets on his mobile. He thinks some of them might be useful."

"Where is he?"

"He works at a burger bar in the shopping centre. He's there until six."

He looked around at the forensics people still hard at work. "Okay, we'll go and talk to him."

* * *

"What are you doing, Neville?"

"Washing the blood off my knife."

"Did you cut yourself? How many times have I told you to be careful with that damn thing?"

"I've done something," he said. He turned round to look at the man. "The voices said it was okay. Promise you won't shout."

"Spit it out, Neville."

"I got rid of Dan. He was being a right pain in the arse. I lost my rag with him." Neville cowered at the sink, waiting for the shouting to start.

"You've been out?" *He* asked incredulously, "when I expressly told you not to?"

"I got bored."

"So you went out and jumped that friend of yours instead?"

"He's no friend. He called me names and he wanted me to take his pills. I'm done with all that."

"Is he badly hurt?"

"Yeah. Think he's dead."

Neville watched him, trembling, as *he* ranted around the house, shouting and throwing things. Finally *he* lashed out and landed Neville one on the chin. Neville stumbled backwards and fell to the floor.

"You're a bloody fool! They'll be onto you." *He* drew aside a curtain and looked up and down the street. "If the police come knocking, you're on your own."

"You'll stick up for me, though? You won't let them lock me away. It was only Dan. He was a waste of space anyway."

"That's not how they'll see it — idiot!"

He brought his face up close to Neville's.

"They'll haul you away. They'll stick you in a cell and throw away the fucking key!"

"You shouldn't have left me on my own."

"I have to work. Who do you think puts food on the table?"

"I've had enough. This isn't fun anymore. You don't let me do anything. I don't see what difference it makes anyway. I did the girls."

"That was different. They won't get you for that. They can't. There's no evidence. Get out of my sight. I need to think."

Neville sloped off to his room. *He* was still pacing the floor. It'd been a pig of a day. Neville couldn't take any more. He wanted to get out. He'd wait until *he* had gone to bed, then he'd do a runner.

* * *

They sat down in an alcove. The empty burger bar smelled of grease and onions. Greco couldn't help looking at the tabletops. They were grimy, sticky and chipped at the edges. He could never eat in a place like this — no matter how hungry he got. Outside, the pavement was littered with food wrappers and polystyrene boxes.

"She goes there a lot. I don't know why. It's nothing but a meat market. I often take photos. She doesn't seem to mind." Dale Fuller got out his phone and showed Greco the images of Jenna Proctor posing for the camera. Greco noticed he was speaking of Jenna in the present tense. It hadn't sunk in.

"The other night I took one or two videos of her dancing. I wanted to ask her out . . . but her friends were always hanging around and I didn't get a chance. She was lovely. I've thought so ever since school. She would probably have said no anyway. Jenna was way out of my league."

111

"Did you take any pictures of her outside?" Grace asked.

He fiddled with the phone for a moment or two and then showed them a short video of Jenna smoking in the doorway with another girl. It must have been cold: the girls were huddled together under a coat.

"Where were you standing when you took this?"

"I went outside with them and stood across the road. I was photographing Jenna, but I'm also doing a project for college. I'm not sure what I'll do now, with Jenna being dead. Her folks might not want me to feature her in it."

"Was there anyone else hanging around, watching the girls or the club?"

"I only had eyes for Jenna. My camera was always pointed her way. But there was this . . . which is why I rang you."

He'd caught the bouncer throwing Jenna's bag and shoes out onto the street.

"That one's a real louse. He's always on at the girls about taking off their shoes and stuff. He didn't like Jenna, or her mates. Whenever they were in he'd pick on them. I was going to show this to the manager. Get him on the bouncer's case."

Greco and Grace could see Jenna on her knees — that would have been when she threw up. But there was a light to the left of her, the headlights of a parked car.

"It might be possible for one of the techies to clean this up, sir, and get a registration number.

"You were standing inside when you took these?"

"Yes, just behind the lout who threw her out."

"Why didn't you say something then? Go out to help her?"

"I wish I had now." He hung his head. "But Jenna was always getting thrown out. She wasn't in a good mood and the bouncer was on my case the minute he saw me taking the photos."

"Did he threaten you?"

"No . . . but he did grab my arm and push me back inside. One of Jenna's mates asked me where she'd gone. I told her. To be honest, I expected her to go and sort her."

"Thanks, Dale. These could be a great help. Can you send them to me from your phone?" Greco tapped his number and email into the boy's phone. "If anything else occurs to you, ring me."

When they were outside, Greco brushed himself down. "I can't understand how places like that stay in business."

"The kids like them, that's why," she told him. "Fast food, meeting up. When you're in your teens, that's what it's all about."

His phone pinged. Dale had sent the photos to him. "I'm going to the station to give these to George if she's still there."

"I'll go home if you don't need me."

"Okay, Grace. See you in the morning."

* * *

Neither Craig nor Speedy were in the office, but George was still hard at it.

He passed her his phone. "Have a look at these. They are images and video of Jenna Proctor at the club. There is a car parked near to where she was pushed out. See what you can do."

George transferred the images and handed the phone back to him. "Something's happened, sir, this afternoon."

About to head off, Greco stopped. "Important?"

"Strange — and that probably makes it important."

"Go on then, tell me."

"We're being talked about on social media — Twitter mostly. These have been circulating since lunchtime, but I've only just seen them."

Greco looked at the string of messages on the screen. There were dozens of them, all from someone calling himself 'smiley mouth.'

"They're aimed at us, sir. Some are criticising the way the investigation is going, some are goading us — betting we won't get him. That sort of thing."

"Anything specific about the murders?"

"No. But that name he's using. I'm thinking about the way he cut their faces."

She was right. "Can we find out who's posting them?"

"I tried, but I've had to pass it up to the techie people. The tweets are bounced around from one IP address to another before they get to us. It's like trying to unravel knitting wool the cat's had hold of."

"The letter sent to Laycock was signed the same way."

"Hashtag 'smiley mouth' is trending, sir. He's getting more followers by the minute."

Chapter 12

Greco didn't want to go home. The last thing he wanted was to end up arguing with Suzy. He could go to his flat, spend the night there. But for once he didn't feel like being on his own.

He left his car in the station car park and walked the few hundred yards into Oldston town centre. It was gone seven in the evening so the shops were closed, but the town was still busy. It was a warm evening. People were sitting outside the pubs, drinking. Everyone looked so happy, without a care in the world. Didn't they realise they had a monster in their midst?

He crossed the High Street and went into the Crown. He needed a drink. He wasn't a regular pub-goer and didn't know the pubs in Oldston, but he had been in there. If he did drink, he usually preferred to do it at home. But not tonight.

Megan Hunter greeted him with a wary smile. "Your people were in earlier," she told him. "I've nothing else to say."

"I'm not working," he said. "Give me a whiskey, please."

Her face softened. "Hard day?"

He nodded.

"Shame. You're all alone. Couldn't you persuade Grace to join you?"

"We're work colleagues," he said.

"You could do worse, you know." She put down his drink. "She's an attractive woman — and single."

Ignoring her comment, Greco swallowed the whiskey. He'd never been a big drinker but this one hardly touched the sides. "Another, please."

"Well, if it isn't one of our inept policemen!" The voice came from behind, startling him. "I'm surprised you've got time to drink, Inspector. That murdering bastard is still on the loose. Shouldn't you be somewhere else?"

Laycock.

"I'm having a quiet drink. I suggest you go and bother someone else," he said, keeping his voice even.

Laycock laughed. He clapped Greco on the back, affably. "Have you eaten? I don't know if you're aware of it, but this pub is famous for its meat-and-potato pie. There's a table free over there."

Megan Hunter was hovering, waiting for him to make up his mind. Greco had hardly eaten all day.

"Okay," he said, wearily.

"You grab the table and I'll get more drinks in."

Drinking with Laycock in the Crown was the last thing he'd expected to be doing. But perhaps he could work it to his advantage. For a start, he wanted to know why the reporter was so down on the police.

As Greco sat waiting for him to bring the drinks over, he checked Twitter on his phone. There were another half dozen or so scathing missives. He'd have a closer look later and try to analyse the content. For now he had Laycock to contend with.

He took his whiskey and made himself comfortable. The place wasn't bad. It looked clean at least. They were sitting in the designated eating area. All the tables were covered with crisp white tablecloths and had a small posy of flowers in the centre. Ordinarily he'd think twice before eating anywhere that didn't have its current hygiene certificate on display. But this place *felt* okay, and Grace had said Megan Hunter had worked hard to turn the place around.

"He isn't giving much away, your killer." Laycock said, after swallowing half of his pint.

"You can't possibly know that," Greco replied.

"Get off it! He's got you stumped. Admit it — this bastard's clever."

"They're never that clever, believe me. We've got one or two strong leads."

"He's leading you up the garden path, you mean. This one's a planner. He's got you lot floundering around chasing your tails."

"Why are you so against us? A different attitude could pay dividends, you know."

"What do you mean?"

"The press could help. You could encourage people to come forward, tell us what they know."

"This is too big for you to handle," said Laycock. "There was supposed to be a special squad set up to deal with cases like this. Where is it? What's happened to all the big plans we were told about in that press release three months ago?"

"It takes time. The powers that be haven't found the right people yet."

"Look, Greco, this isn't personal. I see a story and I go after it."

"You turn it into a circus, you mean. You twist things, tell lies. You accomplish nothing and upset people. It was you who spoke to Mavis Weston and told her a pack of lies about what had happened to her daughter."

"Fine. If all I'm going to get is grief, you can go and sit somewhere else, Greco."

"That woman had just heard that her daughter had been murdered. You came along and stuck the knife in even deeper. What did you tell her, Laycock?"

"The truth."

"And what truth was that?"

"Whatever my readers want to read. I sell papers. A story like this one sells thousands."

"You're a louse. Do you know that?"

"Sorry, can't help it."

This wasn't a chance meeting, Greco suddenly realised. Laycock wanted something.

"The story is everything. And this one is big." He paused, regarding Greco closely. "When are you going to let us in, Mister Policeman? Why won't you tell us the truth?"

"We can't. It's not that sort of case," said Greco.

"What if we do an exchange? We'll give you the help you talked about and you give us more information. We could run an appeal. Pitch it so that folk would come forward."

Greco shook his head. "Absolutely not. We cannot release any details. Besides, in my experience, people around here are very reluctant to help the police in any way — murder or no murder.

"They might loosen their tongues for a reward. My paper would help," Laycock said. "It's surprising what people will do for money."

"Not this time."

"I think you're wrong."

Megan Hunter chose that moment to serve the food. Greco had to calm down enough to eat it. He took another slug of whiskey. "Would you bring me a half?"

They ate in silence. Laycock had been right about one thing. The pie was good. Greco washed it down with his beer.

"Hope you're not driving home, Inspector."

"Don't worry about me, Laycock."

Laycock laughed. "Well, riveting as this is, I've got to go. There's a taxi rank round the corner if you need one. Wish I could say it had been a pleasure, but we both know that would be stretching it."

Greco watched as he picked up his stuff and left. He'd give him a few minutes then get off himself.

But off where? He still hadn't decided. A battle with Suzy, or an empty flat? He found himself out on the street and walking towards Pierce Street. It was getting dark. He tried to do some thinking about the case.

But his mind kept straying back to Suzy, and her tryst in the park. Who was he? Greco had only seen his back. All he could say about his rival was that he was tall with dark hair. She must know him from somewhere — the college where she worked? Suzy had never spoken about anyone there. But then she wouldn't, would she? He needed to speak to her, but not yet. It was all far too raw.

Greco had walked for a good fifteen minutes before he realised he'd taken a wrong turn somewhere. He was nowhere near Pierce Street. His head full of Suzy, he'd wandered aimlessly around the back streets of Oldston. Now he was lost.

He walked another hundred yards or so and saw a street sign. This was where Grace lived.

He hadn't done it on purpose. He was confused. The drink, the shock of Suzy, and the case. At least Grace would understand. He rang the front doorbell.

"Sir! Something happened?"

"Call me Stephen and yes, I suppose it has."

* * *

"Coffee and toast will have to do you."

Grace came into the sitting room where Greco lay on the sofa, still half asleep.

"Fine." He winced at the rattle of crockery on the table. His head hurt.

"Me too," Grace said. She moved his legs aside so she could sit down. "We got talking and I opened a bottle of red. You must have had quite a mix last night."

He couldn't remember.

"What did I say?"

"You ranted a bit about Laycock. You told me your ex-wife is having an affair, and how pissed off you are about it."

He must have really opened up. Not like him. Greco brushed his hair back from his forehead. He still hadn't got it cut. "I'm sorry, Grace. I don't know why I came here, but it was good of you to let me stay."

"Just as well you did. You were drunk. You were quite funny, actually," she giggled.

"Not my usual style."

"What, being funny?"

"No — sleeping on colleagues' sofas."

"It's better than crashing on some bench somewhere."

"Do you mind if we keep this to ourselves?" This was way off beam for him. Greco couldn't remember the last time he'd got drunk. He didn't think he'd ever behaved this way with a female colleague.

"Fine by me." She passed him the coffee. "Why — am I that embarrassing?"

"It's nothing like that. I just feel such a fool. This isn't the way I carry on, believe me. Seeing Suzy with another man — it shook me up. I went a bit crazy for a while. It was so unexpected. After all, it was her that wanted to try again."

"Yes I know — you told me. In fact you wouldn't shut up. You gave me chapter and verse." She winked at him. "You also told me to call you 'Stephen.' But perhaps not when we're on duty, eh, sir."

Grace was grinning. What else had he said? And even more worrying — how had he behaved? Time to get out of there.

"Can I use your shower?"

"Help yourself. Clean towels are on the shelf in the bathroom. Make as much noise as you want. You won't wake anyone up. My mum came for Holly ages ago."

"She saw me — here?"

"She didn't bat an eye," Grace teased. "She's well used to me bringing men home."

Greco looked horrified.

"Joke, sir. I told her you had problems. She understood."

"I've overstepped the mark." He sat up.

"No, you haven't. You needed someone to talk to. I don't mind being your sounding board."

"I don't want this getting around the station."

"I won't say a word," she promised. "Given that we're sharing confidences, I'll let you in on a little secret. I've started seeing someone."

Greco smiled. That was good. Grace deserved to be happy.

"It's still early on in the relationship but I like him and so does Holly. I don't want folk at the station gossiping about me, either."

"Do I know him?"

"You might actually, but that's all I'm saying."

He checked his watch. "It's nearly nine."

"I know, and we're late for work."

Chapter 13

George was addressing the team, showing them the tweets that had been posted overnight.

"They are getting more specific. Yesterday it was just general stuff. How badly the investigation was going. How we'd never catch the killer because we are all stupid, that sort of thing. But today the tone has changed."

"See?" She pointed to one of them.

"He mentions the face cutting," Greco said.

"So what are we saying? That these are from him — the killer?" Speedy asked.

"Can't we find out who sent them?" Craig said.

"The techie people are hard at it," George told them. "But they're having the same problem I had and it's going to take a while."

"Apart from these, where are we up to?"

"Some of the forensics are in, sir," Craig said. "The blood on the safe did not belong to Jenna Proctor but they have no match on file."

Greco groaned. He had hoped the blood would yield something. "The cameras at the house?"

"Nothing. Not a flutter. The killer hasn't been back."

"We got the tox report for both girls. They'd both been given a high dose of tranquiliser. Enough to make them unaware of their surroundings," George said.

Greco had suspected as much. It was a blessing of sorts, given what was done to them. "Anything interesting on Jenna's phone?"

"The Duggan sent through what they could from the sim card, but the fire damage was too extensive. They got her history from the service provider. I've printed out copies for everyone," George said.

It was the usual stuff, teenage angst and a host of acronyms. Greco had no idea what most of it meant.

"We got a partial car registration from one of the videos Dan Fuller gave us. We're trying to match it to something local."

That would take time too. "What else are we still waiting for?"

"The prints on the beer can, sir," Speedy replied. "The one I pulled out of the bin in the park. It might be an idea to look at the care home a little closer. There could be something in the theory that the killer has a link with it. He knows how things work — the key safes for example. He knows where the new residents lived previously. He can tell which of those houses will suit his purpose."

He was right.

"Speak to the nurse, Lorraine Hopkirk, and also the manager," Greco said. "See what you can turn up."

"Sir!" Grace called out. "The papers are in. You should look at this."

Greco took the tabloid she held out for him. It was one of the nationals. There, on the front page was a piece by Oliver Laycock. He had written in lurid detail about the killings and once again he'd pulled the police apart for their lack of action.

Greco sank into his chair. This was all he needed. This morning the nationals — and tonight?

"Stephen!" DCI Green came in.

"You've seen this, sir?" He passed him the paper.

"I've just had the super on. He wants a meeting — you, me and him. It won't be pleasant. The editor of that rag contacted him earlier."

"We are doing everything we can, sir. The Duggan are working flat out on every bit of evidence we send their way. But none of it leads anywhere."

"Can you produce a short report? Wilkes wants us in his office at four this afternoon."

Greco nodded.

Once the DCI had left, Greco addressed the team. "You all heard that."

"We're doing our level best." Speedy shook his head. "That man wants to try it. Things have changed since his day. Villains are more forensically aware. They don't make the mistakes they used to."

"But he has made mistakes," George reminded him. "The blood on the safe, the footprint, playing loud music that half the street heard. The fact that he's been seen by the neighbours and they are able to describe him — it all adds up."

"George has a point . . ."

Greco suddenly recalled what Laycock had said — *this one was a planner.* "But they're not mistakes. These so-called mistakes are deliberate. He's been leading us on. Planting stuff for us to find."

"Why? I don't see the point."

"Neither do I, Speedy, but he'll have one."

"Inspector Greco?"

They all turned round. A woman was standing in the doorway. The team fell silent, looking at her. She was tall and slim, but the most outstanding thing about her was her long glossy black hair. Despite an attempt to pin it back it hung in soft waves, framing her face. The hair turned an attractive woman into a stunner.

"DS Scarlett Seddon from Daneside." She smiled at them.

He finally found his tongue. "I'm Greco."

"Sorry I couldn't get here sooner. You know how these things are. We've had a series of armed robberies to deal with."

Green had mentioned help from Daneside but the DCI hadn't updated him since then. Greco wondered if a DS from outside would help or hinder the investigation.

"We were going over what we've got so far," he said. "Come in and join us." He pointed towards the incident board. "I don't know if you've been briefed or not. We suspect a serial killer. Two murders, both the same MO."

"All I was told was that you're up against it. I'll read the reports, get up to speed."

"I'm DC Grace Harper." Grace stepped forward and held out her hand. "If you want anything, just ask."

"You can have that desk. It's going spare," Craig said.

"Do you have any suspects?"

"No. He's careful. We were just discussing the probability that he's leaving a false trail. He wants us running around chasing our tails."

"Sounds personal."

Greco hadn't considered that one. Perhaps a fresh face with new ideas wasn't such a bad idea after all. He introduced his team.

"That's DS Quickenden, DC Merrick and Georgina Booth, our information officer. They're not a bad bunch — and friendly. They'll fill you in with what you need to know." He paused. "Can I suggest that for today you work with Grace?"

She nodded.

It wouldn't be a good idea to put her with Speedy just yet. He knew what would happen. Speedy needed his mind on the case, not on the new DS.

"Craig? You and George continue looking for the car that goes with that partial registration. Enter everything we've got so far into the database and see what it spits out. Grace — you and Scarlett attend Dan Roper's PM at the

125

Duggan. While you're there, check if any other results have come in."

"We off to the care home, sir?" said Speedy.

"Yes. Then I'll have to come back and write that report."

* * *

Grace and Scarlett made for the car park. "Have you worked on many murders?" Grace asked.

"A fair few. It's never pleasant. I don't like PMs much either. Pity that's what I get on my first day." She got into the passenger seat.

"This one will be easy compared to what the boss and Speedy have seen this week. The man we're after is a cruel bastard and no mistake."

"Speedy?"

Grace laughed. "The tall thin one with the face and the short hair — DS Quickenden," she said.

"Ah, I see. Quick — Speedy," she laughed. "And what do you mean — the face?"

"I don't know what it is with him, but he just can't get the hair right. It's that long face and those sticky-out features. He had a head full of curls up until about three months ago but the boss made him get it cut."

"What's he like — DI Greco?"

"I find him okay," Grace didn't want Scarlett thinking she was up for gossiping about their boss. "He can come across as a bit odd sometimes. He has a thing about cleanliness and keeping things tidy."

"But he gets the job done and that's what counts."

"Yes, and that's why he's finding this one so hard. We're putting in the graft but we're getting nowhere."

Grace tried to keep the chat light as they drove down the dual carriageway. She didn't want to discuss her colleagues any further.

"You've made sergeant young."

"I'm not that young," Scarlett laughed. "Twenty-five — and it took a lot of hard work, believe me."

"Still, you did it. That's what I want — promotion. It would be great if I could do it within the next couple of years. I need the extra money. I'm the breadwinner in my house. There's only me and my daughter."

"Can't be easy with a child in tow."

"It's not. But I get by with some childcare help from my mum. You got any?"

She shook her head. "And I'm not attached either — just in case you or the others were wondering."

"Here we are — the Duggan Centre. Does your team use this place?"

"No. Daneside hasn't decided if it'll outsource yet."

"Doctor Barrington is the pathologist who'll be doing this one," Grace said as they went in. "The young man was found stabbed in Oldston Park. The reason we're so interested is because a piece of scalp was removed — same as with the girls."

Grace and DS Scarlett Seddon stood on a raised platform looking out over the post-mortem room. The body of Dan Roper was laid on the table, ready for the scalpel.

"Hate these," Scarlett whispered. "All that cutting and the gore. Makes me want to heave."

"Good morning!" Natasha Barrington entered with her assistants. Mark Brough was with her again plus a couple of lab people and the photographer.

"DI Greco alright now? He seemed a little off colour yesterday afternoon in the park."

"He's fine!" Grace called out. "Must have been the lunch he ate. This is DS Scarlett Seddon. She's joining us for a while."

Natasha nodded. "Right, folks, let's get this done."

"Hang on to your stomach," Scarlett said.

"Dan Roper. He was identified by his GP. He was twenty-two years old and had a history of drug abuse. I've done a tox screen. I'll report back when the results are through."

She removed the sheet covering his body. His skin was white, his extremities and lips blue. Grace shivered.

"He has one wound to his chest," Natasha probed with a gloved finger. "The cut is deep." An assistant passed her a scalpel. They watched as she carefully exposed the wound so she could see how deep into the body it went.

"The blade went in deep. It most likely pierced the heart. We'll know that shortly. One stab with force behind it — in and out." She made the movement with her hand. "It will have taken just seconds and his life was over. Apart from that there are no other recent cuts or bruises on his body."

"What about his scalp?" Grace asked.

Natasha moved the hair so she could examine it. "Interesting . . . the skin has been removed in a similar fashion to the girls, but not with the same finesse. Whoever did this was clumsy. The wound is ragged — the skin cut into then torn away. Get a good shot of this," she told the photographer. "Greco will want to compare it with the others."

"Whoever did that knew about the girls?" Scarlett asked.

"We're presuming so. It's an extremely unlikely coincidence."

The pathologist opened up the body and began to remove the internal organs. The detectives could hear a slosh as the wet intestines slithered into a waiting bowl. Grace turned away.

"His heart was damaged beyond repair," the pathologist said, holding it up. "He'd have died within seconds. Interestingly, the direction of the cut is very similar to that of the heated poker. The same area of the heart was destroyed."

"The question is, was this done by the same man? Were there any witnesses at the scene?" Scarlett asked.

"No. A group of lads using the skateboarding rink saw two young men sitting on a nearby bench watching them. They appeared to have an argument. One rushed off and the other gave chase. Unfortunately no one could give a useful description," said Grace.

"Shame."

"That's what we've been up against since the start. No one sees, no one tells. It's as if this man is invisible."

"The report will be on the system later," Natasha said. She left the room.

"The photos will be available sooner," Mark Brough told them. "My colleague will upload them when we're done."

"He seems okay. Easy on the eye too." Scarlett whispered to Grace.

"I don't know anything about him. He could already be seeing someone for all you know."

"Like the DI, you mean. He's got his ex-wife. Doesn't stop you, does it?"

"The images of the crime scene will be in the same folder as the report," Mark said.

"You're new, aren't you?" Scarlett said. She was smiling at him and playing with her hair.

"Yes. I've only been in the job a few weeks. You too, I believe."

"Oh, I'm a lot newer than that. Just this week."

"Perhaps we newbies should get together. Fancy a drink sometime?" Scarlett said.

"I'll leave you to it. I'll wait in the car," Grace said.

* * *

"This is an unexpected treat — lunch out." Suzy Greco smiled as the car door was opened for her.

"You deserve it." He leaned forward and kissed her cheek. "I thought we'd go for a picnic. Drive out to that country park out Leesworth way. Eat fancy sandwiches and drink coffee."

"Sounds okay to me." She took the drink he offered her.

"Sorry it's in one of those carton things. I've got a bottle of wine in the boot."

"Drunk at work. What will the students say?" She giggled. "Nice coffee."

"I went to that new deli place. When we finally come out — you know, tell folk — we'll have to eat there properly. We should do it soon. I can't see any point in holding back."

"Stephen already knows," she told him. "I had no choice but to say something. He saw us in the park yesterday."

"He knows who I am?"

"No, and I didn't tell him. He saw me but he couldn't see you properly. He was there looking into some assault, I think."

"There was some sort of fight in the park yesterday. A bloke was carted off in an ambulance."

"Stephen came home in the afternoon and we spoke. He's confused about what's going on. He'll get over it. He did the last time we split. He didn't come home last night. He'll have gone to that flat of his to lick his wounds."

"So I've got him worried, have I?"

"This isn't a game, you know. I might be seeing you, but Stephen has to remain in our lives, mine and Matilda's. I can't cut him out completely. You do understand that? This is fun — but we don't have to get too heavy. Let's take it slow. See where it goes."

"Anything you want. Anyway, you know what I think. That man deserves all he gets. He's like all the rest. It's all about the job, and nothing else matters. He barely notices you, Suzy. You're both young. You should be enjoying life as a family. Instead he spends his time up to his armpits in villains and leaves you to raise the kid and keep house. You could have so much more out of life."

Suzy scrunched up the carton and put it in a carrier bag on the floor of car. She yawned and leaned back. "I'm well aware of Stephen's flaws. But he's a good man. Don't be so hard on him." She yawned again.

"Tired, sweetheart?"

"Don't know what's come over me. I can't keep my eyes open."

"Slip the seat back. Close your eyes for five minutes. We'll be there soon."

Chapter 14

"That got us nowhere." DS Jed Quickenden kicked a tyre of the pool car they were using. "A list! What good is a flaming list?"

"Lorraine Hopkirk needs time to think it through. If there is someone working at the home who could have taken those keys, she'll tell us. She's a bright woman."

"Well, she's told us nothing so far."

Greco looked around at the large Victorian houses and well-tended gardens. "This is a pleasant area."

"The posh end of town." Speedy grinned.

"Shame they don't appreciate it." Greco nodded towards a group of youths who were shouting obscenities. Their target was a figure standing in the window of a house beside the care home.

"That place comes in for a lot of stick. It's Springbank — a place for dropouts."

"What sort of dropouts?"

"Ex drug-users, psychiatric cases. You name it, they all go there. The local residents don't like it. They objected when it was first set up but they got nowhere."

"Has there ever been any trouble?"

"Nothing that we've had to get involved with."

"So the people that run it do a good job then?"

Speedy shrugged. "What now, boss?"

"There's something I've got to do." Greco was thinking about Doris Hope. He hadn't dropped her wages off yet and he hadn't told her about the cameras he'd had fitted at the house in Pierce Street either.

"You take the car and get back to the station. I'll join you in a while."

"Don't you need a lift, sir?"

"No — I'll walk. I'm not going far."

Greco still felt rough from the previous night's drinking. His head had been thumping all day. He couldn't think clearly. A walk might help.

Doris Hope didn't live far from the town centre. It shouldn't take long. Once he sorted that, he'd go back and write the report for the super. It was a pity he had nothing new to add. Everything the super and the DCI needed to know was up on the incident board.

* * *

"Cup of tea?" Doris Hope offered when she saw him on the doorstep.

Greco nodded, and followed her into a narrow hallway.

"Sit down in there and I'll put the kettle on."

The sitting room she showed him to was small and full of furniture. But there wasn't a speck of dust or a thing out of place. Even the cushions on the sofa had been placed just so.

"It won't be a minute," she said.

"I came to give you this." He handed her an envelope. "Also to tell you something about the house you're buying on Pierce Street."

"I know about that," she said with a frown. "My Albert bumped into one of your policemen. He'd been keeping an eye open. He told him about the cameras inside."

"We'll remove them as soon as we can."

"It's not that." She sat down opposite him. "It's the idea that something so awful could happen in there. We couldn't keep the house if it did. I would never feel right inside there again."

"It seems unlikely now. Whoever is doing this has more than likely been scared off," he said.

"I hope Albert didn't do any damage to anything. He was moving stuff about early this morning. He's been getting everything ready to make a start."

"Don't worry. The cameras have been placed well out of harm's way."

* * *

It was nearly four when Greco got back to the station. The team were hard at it, including Scarlett.

"There are over a hundred cars in Oldston with those letters in their registration, sir," she said.

It was a thankless task. "Anything else come in?"

"A shed load more tweets," Speedy said. "But still nothing from the clever boys upstairs."

Greco's phone rang.

"Mr Greco? It's Mrs Halshaw from the Duke Academy. Matilda is still here. Her mother hasn't picked her up yet. Is anything wrong?"

"Not that I'm aware of," he said. "I'll try and get hold of her, but if not I'll pick Matilda up myself in about twenty minutes."

"Problem, sir?" Grace said.

"Not sure. Suzy hasn't picked Matilda up from school."

He punched Suzy's work number into the office phone and waited. She wasn't there.

"She left at lunchtime and didn't return," he said to Grace.

"There'll be some reasonable explanation. But you'd better do something about Matilda."

Greco had a good idea what that explanation would be, and from the look on Grace's face, so did she. The new boyfriend. Whoever he was, he'd obviously turned her head. But to forget about picking up their daughter — that was going some.

"Do you want me to go and get her, sir?" Grace was tidying the pile of paperwork on her desk.

He looked at the office clock on the wall. There was that meeting with the super and the DCI. "Would you mind?"

She shook her head. "I'll take her back to mine. Give her some tea with Holly. It'll be a treat for them."

* * *

The man at the door told Neville to wait in the hall while he went to get Edna. The place smelled — tobacco and beer. Someone had been naughty again. Well, no one could blame Neville. He hadn't even been here. He'd been asleep all night and most of today. *He* must have given him some pills. He'd have to be careful in future — watch what he swallowed. His head was buzzing with everything that had happened. He really needed to talk to Edna. She'd know what to do.

"Neville!"

Her voice was comforting. It washed through him. All the anxiety went away. He wished he could stay here all the time. He'd be safe then.

"Where have you been?"

She sat down beside him. She was wearing her nurse's uniform.

"You've missed all your appointments this week. Have you been unwell?"

"No." Neville shook his head guiltily.

"You should have seen Doctor Fielding yesterday afternoon. Where were you?"

"I forgot."

"We wrote it down. You even put everything into your phone. Don't you remember that?"

He'd found it and deleted the lot. Now Neville was in trouble.

"It wasn't me," he said.

Edna fixed him with a look. She didn't believe him. He could tell she thought it was happening again. He squirmed in the chair.

"It really wasn't me. *He* did it. I'm not allowed to do anything without *his* say-so. I'm surprised *he* even lets me breathe these days."

The words were out before he could stop them. Now she really would think he was ill again.

"Doctor Fielding is in this afternoon."

He knew it. She'd got the wrong end of the stick.

"Stay, Neville. Just speak to him."

"No. *He'll* want to keep me here like before. I've got to go."

Neville stood up. Coming here was a mistake. He could see that now. Edna didn't understand him anymore. How come? Had *he* spoken to her? Shopped him? Had *he* made Edna believe he was bad? Neville didn't want Edna thinking that.

"Has something happened? Stop pacing about and come and sit down again."

Neville knew he had to be careful what he said, but the words wanted to come out.

"Something did happen, but I'm okay now," he said. "Dan won't bother me again, so I'll be fine." Why had he mentioned Dan? Too late now — it was out. "In fact he won't bother anyone again. Poor Dan. He shouldn't have said those things about me. Called me that name." Neville was staring at his feet.

"Who is Dan?"

"No one now. He's dead."

"Neville? Did you have anything to do with that?"

He shook his head. He wanted to tell her the truth but he couldn't. If he told her about Dan, then he'd have to talk about the girls. She couldn't find out about them. If she did, Edna would hate him.

"Are you sure? Have you hurt somebody?"

Where to start? There was a thundering in his head. He got to his feet and began pacing again. He was wound up, confused, and the thoughts wouldn't go away. A little voice hammered away at him. *Tell her. Tell her, before it's too late — before you hurt someone else.*

He'd had enough.

"I've done something bad." He stopped pacing and hung his head. Edna stood up and put her arm round his shoulder.

"I'll get Doctor Fielding. You wait here. Come on, sit down. It'll only take a minute."

As soon as she left, Neville realised he'd be mad to tell her all that stuff. *He'd* been right. They'd lock him up. He got to his feet, yanked open the front door and did one.

* * *

It was dark. Suzy Greco blinked a few times, trying to clear her eyes. She couldn't remember what had happened. The hours since the morning seemed to have disappeared. Panic gripped her. Where was she? She had to be dreaming. She wasn't properly awake yet. It'd be okay in a moment. She'd wake up properly.

But something was wrong. Her limbs were cold and stiff. Why couldn't she move? When her eyes became accustomed to the gloom, she looked down and saw that her wrists were taped to the arms of a chair, her ankles to its legs. More heavy tape had been wound around her middle to keep her immobile. But worse than that, she was naked. She tried to scream but no noise came.

Chapter 15

Day Four

"My mum will take them both to school. I ran her things through the wash last night with Holly's."

"Thanks. I'm really grateful for what you've done. Tell Matilda I'll be there to pick her up later." He was speaking to Grace on the phone.

"Suzy?"

"I've been trying her mobile all night, but nothing. It's turned off."

"Surely she wouldn't just go off and leave Matilda without saying anything? Sir?"

"Your guess is as good as mine. She's changed recently. I can't read her anymore. If I hadn't seen it with my own eyes, I would never have believed she'd cheat on me with another man."

"Don't worry about Matilda. I'll sort the girls and then come in. How did your meeting go with Wilkes?"

"He wants results. He appreciates we're up against it but like he pointed out — that's the job."

"Did he offer anything that would help?"

"No. Scarlett is the sum total of what we're going to get."

"Well, let's hope we get a breakthrough soon. See you later, sir."

Greco was worried, not only about his daughter but about Suzy's welfare. He'd spent the night wandering around his flat, thinking about her. He didn't believe she'd take off on a whim. She wouldn't do something like that without making arrangements for Matilda. Something had happened, something she had no control over. Reluctantly, he'd rung round all the hospitals on the off-chance she'd been involved in an accident. As the hours ticked by, he wasn't sure if he was pleased that she hadn't been.

He showered and dressed. His first task would be to visit the college. He wanted to know when she'd last been seen, and what sort of mood she'd been in. If he got nothing and she didn't contact him, he'd be forced to ring her parents in case she'd gone there. But that would be a last resort. If she wasn't there, they would only worry.

* * *

On arriving at Oldston College, Greco went up to the staffroom. One of her colleagues, Jill Brayshaw, recognised him.

"Is Suzy here?" he asked her.

"No, and she hasn't rung in either. Is she ill?"

"I don't know. I can't find her," he admitted. "When did you see her last?"

"She was here yesterday morning. She took the National Diploma group." She paused. "Is everything okay with you two? I ask because Suzy's behaviour has been a little odd recently."

"In what way?"

"She's been going out for lunch a lot and dropping hints. We work together and we are quite close. I thought perhaps she was trying to tell me something. I teased her about it. At first I thought she must be meeting you. But that wasn't the case, was it?"

Greco shook his head.

"To be honest, I sort of guessed that she was seeing someone else. She had that look about her — more make-up, always at the hairdressers and she'd been buying new clothes."

How come he hadn't noticed any of that? Perhaps Suzy was right — he was too engrossed in the job.

He saw the flush of embarrassment on her cheeks. "In the end I asked her and Suzy admitted as much."

"Do you know who he was?" he asked.

Jill Brayshaw shook her head. "But I think it must have been him that kept ringing her. She went off at lunchtime yesterday. Said she had something better to do than eat the rubbish they dish up in the canteen. Sorry — I don't know anymore."

"Thanks — it's something to start with anyway."

Greco went downstairs to the reception office. He knew that there was CCTV at the front of the building. He wanted to know exactly when Suzy had left and who she was with.

* * *

"Where's the boss?" DC Scarlett Seddon asked.

"He won't be long," Grace said.

"Right little teacher's pet, aren't you? Running after his kid like that. Do that a lot, do you?"

"It isn't like that."

"Oh, it is." Craig Merrick butted in. "She fancies the pants off him, but he isn't having any."

Scarlett giggled. "That's how you intend to climb up the greasy pole, is it?"

"You're one to talk. What about you and that new bloke at the Duggan? Threw yourself at him, you did. Shameless piece of work!"

"Pack it in you lot. We've got stuff to do, remember?" Speedy was trying to concentrate. He was going through the report George had printed out for them earlier.

"Results of the prints on that beer can are in. No match on the database," said George.

Speedy threw his pen onto the desk and stood up. "What is it with this bastard? No one's that good."

"Well, this one is. He's someone new and he's got no record," said Scarlett.

"That doesn't help."

"Would you like me to go over the reports and the statements? A fresh pair of eyes," she said.

"If you want to, but we should be out there."

"If we knew what it was we were looking for," Merrick added. "The press are right. We haven't got a clue."

"In that case we need to up our game. You didn't see those girls." Speedy shuddered. "Bloody maniac."

"Anything on the tweets?" Grace asked George.

"Nope. They're still working on them."

"Tell them to get a bloody move on. Don't they know what we're dealing with?" Speedy said.

Grace's mobile beeped. It was Greco. He'd sent her a text to say he'd be late in. He was looking at CCTV footage at the college.

"I think the boss has a problem," she said to the others.

"What problem?" Merrick asked.

"He'll tell you himself."

Speedy saw Scarlett and Merrick exchange looks. This was how gossip started. "Spit it out or keep it to yourself," he snapped at Grace. "We don't have time for this bickering. We need to find something we can work with." He held up a file and shook it at them. "Before this character does it again."

Grace was annoyed with him. Speedy could see it on her face. The atmosphere in the office was tense. She'd just opened her mouth to retaliate when a uniformed officer stuck his head around the door.

"We've got a bloke downstairs who says he's responsible for killing those girls."

"It'll be a bloody weirdo," said Speedy. "As if we didn't have enough to do."

"You'll still have to see him though," said Grace. "Greco won't be in for a while, so it's down to you."

Speedy strode off after the officer. He needed a break from the incident room anyway. "What have you done with him?"

"I've stuck him in an interview room. I've left someone on watch."

"Waste of time. This is how it gets sometimes. Every now and again we have a case that attracts the dross." Speedy was only surprised there hadn't been more.

Speedy observed the young man through the two-way glass. He was young, twenty-one or so, and big — at least six foot, and hefty with it. He looked dirty, unshaven and was scruffily dressed in jeans and a hooded top. He looked as if he'd been sleeping rough.

"He's after a hot meal and a bed for the night," Speedy said. He'd seen it before. They got any number of homeless chancing their arm. "What's he said?"

"Nothing to us. Wants to speak to CID only."

Speedy shook his head. This was a waste of time. He went into the room and sat down opposite the man with a notepad and pen in his hand.

"What's your name?"

"Does that matter?"

"Yes, it does." Here we go, thought Speedy. The dragging it out, the fairy tales leading to endless cups of coffee and eventually, if this lad was lucky, a room for the night. "Look, have you got anything to tell me or not?"

"I'm here, aren't I?"

He looked Speedy in the face. His eyes were wild, bloodshot, and he was nervous. He played with the frayed edge of a cuff on his hoody constantly as he spoke, winding the thread around his finger.

"I didn't want to. It was the voices." He leaned forward. "You've no idea how they get."

He'd been right, thought Speedy. Nutjob.

"The girls," he said. "How did you meet them?"

"They were there, at the houses."

"Yes, but where did they come from?"

"I dunno."

"If you are responsible for their deaths you must know." Speedy paused, watching the confusion on the lad's face. "This is a wind-up, isn't it? You know bugger all."

"The voice said I killed them."

"The voice could be wrong."

"No. It was me. I made a mistake, you see. I only wanted to kill their hearts. They didn't love me. Love comes from the heart, doesn't it?"

"Tell me how you did that — killed their hearts?" Faint bells began to ring in Speedy's brain.

"It was easy. I just stuck the hot poker in deep."

* * *

"You okay, sir? You look a bit rough if you don't mind me saying."

"I've got a lot on, Craig," he said.

"Speedy is downstairs interviewing a bloke who's come in and confessed," Grace told him. "He thinks it's a joke, but you never know."

Greco wasn't listening. He'd logged onto his computer and was accessing his email. The man in the security lodge at the college had promised to seek out yesterday's video and email him a copy. There it was in his inbox.

He studied the video. It showed the usual comings and goings of dozens of students through the main entrance. He moved it forward to about twelve noon —

143

the time Suzy would normally break for lunch. A van pulled up outside. He watched the security man wave it in. Then he spotted it. A dark blue Ford Focus.

Greco began to sweat. He tore at his tie, loosening it. The thing was choking him. This wasn't good. He couldn't see the man's face, the sun was shining on the car's windscreen. But he did see Suzy walk out of the entrance. She waved, smiling at the driver. Suzy obviously knew him. He opened the passenger side window and they spoke for a few moments. All Greco could see was the back of his head. Finally Suzy laughed and got in beside him.

The panic was back. Suzy was in mortal danger. For reasons he couldn't work out, the killer had targeted her.

"How are you doing with the car?" His voice was raspy, the words sticking in his throat.

"No luck yet, sir," Craig replied.

Greco looked at the film again. The full registration was visible. Why hadn't he spotted it moments ago? Because he'd only seen Suzy, that was why. He jotted it down on a piece of paper and handed it over. "Try that." He didn't explain. As Craig was about to open his mouth, Greco silenced him. "Just get on with it. I want to know who owns that car — now."

Chapter 16

"I've had him taken to the cells," Speedy told Greco. "At first I thought he was a hoaxer, but after what he said I don't think he is. He told me what he'd done to the hearts. He even mentioned the poker. He's also given me this." He held up a mobile phone. "I think it was used to send those tweets. I'll get it to the techies, see what they think."

"What's he like?" said Greco. Coupled with the sighting of the car, this was finally something they could use.

"He's not what I expected. He's nervous as hell, frightened of his own shadow. And a bit on the odd side. Says he hears voices."

Greco sighed. "Is he saying the voices made him do it?"

"Yep, that's it. *It wasn't me — they told me to.* You know the type."

"We'll have to speak to him properly, but the thing with the voices could complicate the issue."

"What are you thinking, boss?"

"These voices — he could be schizophrenic. If that's the case, we can't interview him again unless an appropriate adult is present."

145

"Want me to ask him?"

"What do we know about him already?"

"Nothing, other than that he killed the girls because the voices made him."

"Have him taken to the soft interview room. Tell uniform to watch him like a hawk. Get him some tea and I'll have a word."

It was frustrating but, schizophrenic or not, he obviously knew something. Greco went back to the incident room. "Grace, I'm about to talk to that young man about the case. I want you in on it. Five minutes, okay?"

Grace nodded.

Greco left the room, walked down the corridor and knocked on DCI Green's door. Something was niggling him but he couldn't put his finger on it. It wasn't Suzy. Suzy was no niggle. The fact she was missing was huge. He was overtired. He'd hardly slept a wink in two nights, and it was taking its toll. His mind was not as sharp as it should be.

"The custody officer has just rung me," Green said.

"That's not why I'm here, sir. I think whoever took those girls has taken Suzy. She's missing. No one has heard from her since yesterday lunchtime."

Green got to his feet. "What makes you think that?"

Greco told him about the Focus. "It was seen at the club and forensics is looking at paint scrapings from one that left Arnold Street in a hurry."

"Has this got anything to do with the young man in custody?"

"We know nothing about him other than he's confessed, and he does know pertinent details about the killings."

"If he is implicated, you can't be involved in the interviewing."

"I have to talk to him. I need to know if he's seen Suzy. It could be her only chance."

Green paused. "Despite what he's said, he could be fantasising. He could have spoken to someone from the press, overheard something. He still might not be genuine. And you don't know his name?"

"Not yet, sir."

"Okay, speak to him. But if you think he really does have anything to do with the murders, then you back off — understand?"

Greco nodded.

"And make sure you follow procedure to the letter."

* * *

"This is Grace," Greco said, "and I'm Stephen."

He watched the lad's eyes swing to Grace. He was looking at her hair, her face.

"You coppers?"

"Yes. We want to have a chat." Greco smiled. "Drink your tea. There's more if you want it."

Neville smiled. He liked that. Edna always kept the tea coming. "You're pretty for a copper," he told Grace shyly.

"What's your name?" she said gently.

"Promise not to laugh?"

Grace nodded.

"Neville. Neville Dakin. I get a lot of stick because of my name. They call me Naff Nev." He hung his head.

"We're not like that," she said.

"Neville, you told our colleague about the voices. Do they bother you a lot?" Greco asked.

He nodded.

"Are they bothering you now?"

Having to tread on eggshells like this was killing Greco.

"A little bit. They don't want me to stay here."

"We can get someone to sit with you while we chat. Someone you know, who knows you — perhaps a friend or a relative. That will make it easier for you," Grace said.

"Can I choose?"

147

She nodded.

"Anyone I want?" He asked, looking surprised.

"Yes."

"Can Edna come? She won't mind."

"Where can we find Edna, Neville?" Greco asked.

"Springbank House. It's near the park."

"Yes, I know where it is," Greco told him.

"We'll leave you with the officer stood over there while we speak to her," said Grace. They left the room.

"What is Springbank House?" Greco asked.

"It's a rehabilitation centre for people with psychiatric problems who have recently left hospital or have ongoing issues. Usually they don't have a stable home life to return to."

"We need to move fast on this. If he's got Suzy, he won't hang about. All this working around his condition is wasting time. I'd like to just beat the truth out of him."

"That is definitely not like you, sir. Are you sure she's actually missing?" Grace asked as they walked back to the office.

"Yes — positive. The CCTV from the college shows her getting into a dark blue Focus."

Grace gasped. "I'm sorry, Stephen," she said. She took hold of his arm. "Look — me and my mum will sort Matilda for you. She was no trouble yesterday. You talk to her later. Tell her that her mummy has gone somewhere — her granny's. She'll understand that."

"And if Suzy doesn't come back? What do I tell her then?"

"One thing at a time, Stephen."

She was right. "Thank you, Grace. I'd be no good around Matilda anyway. I can't sleep, can't eat . . . it's as if I've stopped functioning. I can't even think straight."

"You're going to have to try and get some rest."

"I can't. My head's a mess. I'm missing something and it won't come. It's been bothering me since yesterday."

"Like I said — you need to relax."

148

He gave a hollow laugh. Greco doubted he'd ever relax again. "If it turns out that this is our man, then Green wants me off the case," he told her.

"Because of Suzy?"

"Yes. If he is involved, then I can't be. Keep this and Suzy's disappearance to yourself for now," he said.

"No problem."

"His name is Neville Dakin," Greco told the team once they were back in the main office. "He hears voices." He cleared his throat. "The voices told him to kill those girls."

"And he expects us to believe that?" Craig Merrick asked.

"Until we know different, we have to. We can't interview him properly until he has an appropriate adult with him. He's asked for a woman called Edna from Springbank House." He looked at Scarlett. "Ring the place and find this Edna. If she's free, tell her about him being here and ask if she'll come down. If she's agreeable, would you go and collect her?"

Scarlett nodded.

"We're running out of time. We need a break on this case and at the moment, Neville Dakin is all we've got."

"What about a solicitor, sir?" Merrick asked.

"Get whoever is on duty to come in."

"Can we process him?"

"No. Not yet. But when we do, I want his prints and DNA at the Duggan fast. We can have another look at that boot print too."

* * *

There was a thin strip of light shining through a gap in the curtains. Daytime. But Suzy had no way of knowing what day, or how long she'd been here. She felt hungry and cold. She had a vague recollection of waking once before. She had been taped to a chair then. Now she was lying on her back on the hard floor, still naked. She was uncomfortable. Her arms were fastened to something behind her head.

"Where . . . am I?" Her voice cracked. Her mouth was dry.

Footsteps approached across the floor, then there was a sharp scratch on her thigh. An injection? He didn't speak. He made no noise except to clear his throat. He was standing over her. Suzy felt the goosebumps rise. What would he do next? She was utterly terrified.

He crouched down. His hands were on her body. They traced over the outline of her slim frame, over her breasts and down her thighs. She held her breath. Finally he wrenched her legs apart. Suzy felt his weight on top of her. The bile rose in her throat. She knew what was about to happen and was helpless to stop it.

"Don't!" She cried out. "Don't . . . don't do this. Let me go. Just leave me somewhere." She wriggled beneath him in a useless attempt to get away.

He grabbed her round the throat. His large, male hand was close to squeezing the breath from her body. She couldn't even scream. All she could do was grit her teeth as he forced himself into her.

* * *

The next time Suzy opened her eyes, the strip of light had gone. It must be night. She was no longer lying down. Every bone and muscle in her body ached. She was hanging up by her arms and it was warmer. He'd lit a fire. She could see the flames licking up the chimney.

Chapter 17

"Edna Rowcroft," she said. "I'm a senior psychiatric nurse currently seconded to Springbank from the Meriden Hospital in Manchester." She was in her late fifties. She was plump and had grey hair pinned up in a neat bun.

"DS Seddon will have explained why we asked you to come here?"

"Yes, she did," Edna stuck her nose in the air. "She spent the entire journey fishing, Inspector. I'm not a fool. I will not divulge medical information about our patients."

Greco looked across at Scarlett. She should have realised that. He needed this woman's help. He certainly didn't want her to be antagonised.

"We need to interview Neville formally," Greco explained. "You are the appropriate adult his condition entitles him to. He asked for you specifically. This is Mr Jarvis, the duty solicitor."

"I don't understand what this is about. Is Neville in some sort of trouble?"

"He came in here earlier today and confessed to two very serious crimes."

"Two? When I saw him yesterday he gave me a garbled tale about a friend of his, an ex-patient called Dan Roper. Is that it?"

"He knew Roper?" Greco was surprised. But perhaps he shouldn't be. It would make sense, given the trophies taken from the girls.

"Roper's a bad influence. I've advised him to keep away on many occasions, but Dan was a magnet for Neville."

"Dan Roper was murdered in Oldston Park yesterday. Did he tell you he was responsible?"

"He said a lot of things. Most of it didn't make sense. I'm not sure that's what he meant. He may simply have seen something, heard something. Neville gets confused. Sometimes reality and the ideas in his head get mixed up."

"Neville came here voluntarily. He told my sergeant that he killed two young women."

Edna Rowcroft was visibly shocked. "That's unlikely," she protested. "He isn't violent as a rule. He's on medication that should keep him stable."

"And if he doesn't take it?"

She shook her head.

"Does anyone monitor what he takes?"

"He has regular blood tests. At this stage of Neville's illness that is deemed sufficient."

"Nonetheless he has told us things we cannot ignore. He knows details about the killings that we haven't released. We need to interview him formally — take his fingerprints and a DNA sample. Before that can happen we need the right people in place — you and Mr Jarvis, the duty solicitor."

"He trusts me. I have been assigned to his case since he started his treatment. I'm not sure how he'll be with strangers."

"We'll have to take that chance. Are you happy to start?"

Edna Rowcroft nodded.

When Neville saw her his face lit up. It was clear that he both knew and liked her. "Can I go home now?" he asked.

"We'll leave shortly." She smiled. "First, I want you to do what this policeman tells you."

A young uniformed officer moved forward and took a set of fingerprints and a DNA sample from Neville Dakin.

"Just a minute," Greco said.

"Neville, can I have a look at your shoes?"

The young man held his leg out, looking puzzled.

"Do you always wear these heavy boots?"

"Yeah, they're special. Keep my feet dry."

"Take a boot print too," Greco advised the uniform.

Neville looked at Edna. "Why are they doing all these things? I don't like it."

"It's okay, Neville. We're just going to talk to these people, help them with a problem they've got," she said.

The uniformed officer left the room. Neville Dakin sat between Edna and Jarvis, while Greco and Speedy sat opposite them.

"I don't like this. I don't know them." Neville was cowering in his seat now. "Will they lock me up?"

"It's okay. They just want to have a chat," Edna said.

"They think I've killed someone."

"You told them you had, Neville. Don't you remember?"

He shook his head.

Greco was listening intently. Was this an act? The man who'd planned the killings was organised, meticulous. If Neville Dakin was the killer, then this was some show he was putting on.

"I'm going to show you some photos." Greco opened a folder and placed the images of Jessie Weston and Jenna Proctor on the table in front of Neville. "Do you know these girls?" They were recent photos given to Greco by their families. Both girls were smiling.

153

Neville shrugged. He gave the photos a fleeting glance and turned his eyes to the wall.

"Have a good look. Have you seen either of them before?"

"I think that one was at the house." Without looking away from the wall, he pointed to the image of Jenna Proctor. "She had nice hair. I took some. I put it somewhere safe." A small smile began to curl his lips.

"Did you hurt them?"

"I killed their hearts."

"How, Neville? How did you do that?"

"I burned through them with a hot poker."

Edna Rowcroft gave a little cry and put her hand over her mouth.

"Where did you do this?"

"I told you — at the house."

"Do you know where this house is?"

"Course I do. I'm not stupid."

Greco took another photo from the folder. This one showed Jessie's face, taken after she'd been found.

"Why did you cut her like that?"

Edna Rowcroft flinched and looked away. But Neville stared at the image with ghoulish fascination. He reached out and traced around the wound with his finger as though he was proud of his handiwork.

"The voice said I had to. She wouldn't smile. The voice wanted her to smile, to say thank you for being chosen."

Edna Rowcroft buried her face in her hands.

"Who chose them?"

"The voice did."

"Tell me about the house. Was it yours?"

"No. I don't know whose it was."

"So why go there?"

"It was empty — no one to butt in." His smile broadened. "I liked the girls. They were pretty. They had no clothes on. I had them both." He looked at Edna. "I used a condom though," he said. "No one's getting pregnant."

"I can't do this," whispered Edna to Greco. "Please, I'll have to leave the room."

"Just a few minutes more."

"Have you seen this woman?" He put a photo of Suzy on the table.

Neville shook his head. "No. Not her."

"Are you sure?" Greco asked as calmly as he could manage. He was seething inside, trying to resist the urge to grab hold of this joker and beat the truth out of him.

"I said so, didn't I? Leave me alone." He looked at Edna. "I haven't had my pills."

* * *

Greco looked at the incident board. It didn't make sense. Neville wasn't the man Suzy was seeing. So what was going on?

"He's not our man. It doesn't add up. Yet he knows things. He recognised Jenna. He was able to describe some of what happened. And he says he's put the hair he took somewhere safe. We'll wait for the Duggan before we decide anything."

"Sir," said George. "Dakin doesn't have a driving licence, but the Focus is registered in his name. He must be able to drive."

"Where does he live?"

"He has a room in a hostel that Springbank put him in. It's a halfway house," Speedy said, rolling his eyes. "He's been placed there by a bunch of do-gooders trying to do right and getting it all wrong. The man's a nutter — pure and simple. Even if we do get cut-and-dried evidence, it's highly likely he'll be declared unfit to plead. You heard him in there. He hears voices. From what he said, they dictate everything he does."

"He could be deliberately misleading us — covering up his guilt. We will get expert help. If he is guilty, he won't get away with it."

"I won't hold my breath, sir."

"We need to see that room he lives in and speak to the people there."

"It's off the dual carriageway — the new build near the second roundabout before you hit the industrial estate."

"Right, Speedy — you know where it is, you can drive."

"Is that a good idea?" Grace asked.

"I can't sit around here doing nothing," he told her.

"I'm just thinking about what DCI Green said."

"I'll catch up with him later. Meanwhile, you say nothing."

"What about Edna Rowcroft? What do I do with her?"

"Arrange for someone to take her back."

* * *

"If he didn't do it, how come he knows so much?"

"Because someone told him, or he was there, watching," Greco replied.

"You think he's working with someone?"

"Yes I do. Dakin knows the killer, but whether he's able to tell us anything about him is another matter."

"Do you think he's playing us?" Speedy asked.

"Perhaps. It's difficult to know. If he isn't, then someone very clever is manipulating him."

"He could have anything going on."

"I don't think he's got what it takes to be the one we're after. Setting things up took some organising — getting the keys and all that. Did Dakin strike you as being up to it?"

"He's a nutcase. They're capable of all sorts. You just never know. Properly medicated he could be some sort of genius."

That was unlikely to be the case but Speedy had a point. Neville Dakin had come across as stupid at times, but that could be an act.

"You're looking a bit ropey, if you don't mind me saying, sir."

"I'm not surprised." Greco sighed. "I've got a lot on my mind, and not just the work stuff."

Speedy gave a humourless laugh. "You're not on your own there. I'm a bloody mess. Work doesn't get any easier and the whole town hates me."

"Anyone in particular?"

"The whole bloody lot of them. I can't go in the Spinners anymore. I tried after we finalised the Grady Gibbs thing, but no one would speak to me. They know I'm not to blame and they didn't even like Gibbs much, but someone has to suffer."

"What are you doing about it?"

"To be honest, sir, I'm thinking of ditching the lot — the job, the town, the whole thing. I'd do it too if I had any money. That's the only thing holding me back. But if things get any worse, I just won't care. I'll take to the road, and stuff the lot of them."

Grace had told him that Speedy was down, but Greco hadn't realised it was this bad. "Don't be too hasty," he said. "Give it some time. Try and pick yourself up. Keep at it and work will be okay. You have a future — maybe your own team one day."

"I wouldn't count on that. There are times when my attitude to the job stinks, I know. You've said so yourself often enough."

Underneath everything, Speedy was a good detective. Greco didn't want to lose him. Not to the bleak future he was painting for himself.

"You're doing fine at the moment. You're putting in the hours, doing the work and losing the bad boy image. Let's get this little lot wound up and then we'll talk," Greco said. "We know each other better now. I can see that you are trying. Your appearance, timekeeping, it's all much better since that first case we worked on."

"I'll give it some thought but I can't promise anything. Up until now the force has been my life. It would be hard to leave. But if I can't get my enthusiasm back for the job, that's what I'll have to do."

"Just give it a little longer," Greco advised.

"Okay. I'm up for that."

Speedy parked the car as near to the block as he could get.

"We don't want it trashing," he told Greco. "This place isn't the Link but even so there's some unsavoury characters here."

"How does it work?" Greco asked as they walked towards the main entrance.

"From what I gather, they leave Springbank and other places like it and are given a room here."

"But they're monitored, surely?"

Speedy shrugged. "You know what it's like. There's no money for anything anymore. So who knows?"

The main door was locked. There was a list of names and buttons on a panel to one side. Neville Dakin had room nine. Greco pressed the 'reception' button.

"What do you want?" asked a voice.

"We're police. Open the door."

The door opened with a buzz. A man in overalls met them in the hallway.

"Who is it about?"

"Neville Dakin."

"We haven't seen him for a while. I rang it in to his support worker yesterday."

"Would that be someone at Springbank House?"

158

"Yes. Any problem with Neville and I ring Edna Rowcroft."

"When did you last see him?" Speedy asked.

"Five days ago. He left here with a rucksack."

"Can I ask what you do here?" Greco was looking around the large hallway and the closed doors leading off it. Each door was numbered. At the end of the hall was a large sitting room. The door was open and he could see through to a garden area beyond.

"I keep an eye on everything. There are twelve people here, all male and all recovering from mental illness. They come here because there is nowhere else for them to go. If they want anything, I sort it."

"What sort of anything?" Speedy asked.

"Shopping if they can't go out. Prescriptions fetching from the chemist. Help with applying for jobs . . . anything and everything." He smiled. "But they are encouraged to be independent. This isn't secure accommodation or anything like it. They go where they want and have people round."

"Could we have a look at Neville's room?" They didn't have a warrant but Greco was hoping the bloke would cooperate.

"Is he in trouble?"

"He could be," Greco said.

"Okay. A quick look won't hurt."

The room was on the first floor. It was simply furnished with a bed, a wardrobe, a chest of drawers and an armchair. It had a large window and an en-suite bathroom.

"No TV?" Speedy said.

"No. This one likes his music." He nodded to a radio on the chest. "Plays the thing all the time he does, loud too."

Greco opened the wardrobe door. A black anorak hung there — and nothing else. "He doesn't have much clothing, does he? And there are no photos or knick-knacks."

"They don't stay here long as a rule. We aim to get them on their feet and into work. After that they usually make their own way."

"Did Neville have any visitors?" Speedy asked.

"Not that I ever saw, and I have a flat on the ground floor. There's not a lot happens here that I don't see."

While they were talking Greco had opened the drawers in the chest. A small paper bag sat on its own inside the top one. He took a pair of nitrile gloves from his jacket pocket and put them on.

"Found something, sir?"

Greco carefully opened the bag. Inside was a lock of long blonde hair tied with a pink ribbon. "What's the betting this belonged to Jenna Proctor?"

"It's just hair, sir. There's no scalp attached."

Greco motioned for Speedy to be quiet. "Thanks. I think we've seen everything. We will have to send a forensic team to look at the room," he said.

"Has he done something?"

"We think he has, yes," Greco said. "I doubt Neville will be coming back. Would you lock this room after we leave and let no one in until the team arrive?"

"What about his car?" the caretaker asked.

"Car?" Speedy repeated.

"Yes. Dakin's car. Not that I ever saw him drive it. He used to keep it in the garage round the back. But last night someone took it out and set it alight in the field at the back."

"Show us," Greco said.

The caretaker led them outside the building and pointed to a grassed area behind the garden. "You can't miss it. It's slap bang in the middle. Lit up the sky like a firework display."

"Was it a dark blue Focus?" Speedy asked.

"Yes."

"You told us you see everything that goes on – did you see who took it?"

"No. It was late. I must have been asleep."

"Keep the garage locked too," Greco instructed the man. "I think we need our forensic team to look at this urgently."

Chapter 18

"Are you going to your flat, sir? Only you're welcome to come to mine. You could have a bite to eat, see Matilda."

Greco shook his head. "I'll pop by and speak to Matilda but I won't stay. I couldn't eat anything anyway." He smiled at her. "It was good of you to ask."

"While you were out, we had a Doctor Fielding on the phone from Springbank," Scarlett told him. "He wasn't very happy about Dakin being kept in the cells."

That young man could stay there and rot for all he cared. Right now, all that concerned him was finding who had taken Suzy before it was too late.

"Stall him if he rings again." Greco wanted some time to go through everything they'd got. The office would be quiet once the team had packed up and gone home.

"Stephen? Can I have a word?"

It was DCI Green. Greco knew what he'd want to discuss — whether he remained on this case. He had to stay with it. He needed to be involved. He followed Green down the corridor and into his office.

"Suzy hasn't turned up yet?"

"No, sir."

"Then you should stand down. If you think there's any chance that her disappearance is mixed up with the killings, then you don't have a choice."

"I don't think it is, sir." The lie was so easy it surprised him. "I showed Dakin a photo. He didn't recognise her, but he did recognise Jenna Proctor. So Suzy isn't mixed up in this."

Green accepted this immediately. After all, Greco had never lied to him before.

"So where is she?"

"Suzy is seeing someone else," said Greco. "I saw her with him. We spoke about it the night before she left. I think she's simply gone off with him for a few days."

"I'm sorry, Stephen. Just when you thought you'd patched things up. Do you know who he is?"

Greco had no idea, but he nodded. It was important that Green believed him. "We spoke about it and she told me. She admitted the lot. He's a colleague from work." He'd never realised lying could be so easy. He almost smiled.

"Okay. If you need some time, let me know."

"I need to get on with the case, sir. We may well have a breakthrough very soon."

"Good. It's about time things came together. What about the thing with the car? You said you saw Suzy getting into the one implicated in the murders."

"Coincidence, sir. There are hundreds of that type of car in Oldston. And we've found it now anyway. It was on some spare land at the back of the block Dakin lived in. It's been burned out. I've got forensics on it."

"Good. We might get something from it."

Greco made his way back to the main office and spoke to the team.

"Where are we up to?"

"Doctor Fielding has been on again. He was annoyed. Says it's urgent," said Scarlett.

163

Greco picked up the phone and punched in the number Scarlett had left on his desk.

"Doctor Fielding? DI Greco from Oldston CID. You wanted a word?"

"Edna Rowcroft has returned to Springbank in some distress. You told her that you suspect Neville Dakin of killing two girls. Is that true?"

"Yes, I'm afraid it is. And there are good reasons for our suspicions."

"That's preposterous!" said Fielding. "You don't know him like we do. Dakin is no killer!"

"He knows things about the killings we're investigating that we haven't released to anybody. How do you explain that if he's innocent?"

"He'll have read the papers — seen a headline or something."

"No. He told us things no one else knows. He is involved somehow, and we can't let him go until he tells us the truth."

"Neville's idea of the truth is complicated . . . He won't be happy in the cells either. He needs his medication. Did he have any tablets on him?"

"I'm not sure but I'll find out. If not I'll get the duty doctor to see him."

"Alright. I will come and talk to you and Neville tomorrow morning, first thing."

"Will you be able to tell us about Neville's history or his condition? It might help if we understood. He seemed very confused when we interviewed him today."

"If he agrees, then yes." The call ended.

"The car has been picked up, sir. It was too badly burned for forensics to get anything. They can't even determine if it was the one the paint scrapings came from."

"The skirmish where the wing mirror got knocked off?"

"Yes. It's a pity. That would have definitely put the car in the right area at the right time. Now the good news. Doctor Atkins rushed through the prints. The ones on the beer can and on the poker match Neville Dakin's. Any possible DNA match to the blood found on the wall will take longer."

Craig gave a little cheer. "The bastard can't wriggle out of it now, voices or no voices."

It was progress. Now they had Dakin, they were building evidence fast. But it still didn't make any sense. Greco was convinced that he wasn't a planner. Preparing those houses, making them ready for the killings, had been carried out by someone meticulous. From what he'd seen of Neville Dakin, that wasn't him.

* * *

Now Greco had to face his daughter. He went round to Grace's and explained to Matilda why she couldn't come home. He did as Grace had suggested and said that her mummy had gone to Norfolk. Matilda accepted the excuse at once.

"You should eat something," Grace said. "Starve yourself and you'll be no good to anyone." She pushed a dish into his hand. "It's lasagne. I made two."

Greco took it gratefully. "Thank you, Grace. I'll return the dish. If you need me, I'll be at the house tonight, not my flat. I'm going to have a good look round, see if I can find any clues. I don't like spying on Suzy, but I don't have much choice. There might be something that'll tell me who he is."

"If you need to talk, I'm here," she said.

More than talk, what Greco needed was for this nightmare to end. He had an uneasy feeling. What if she never came back? What if he was already too late?

Driving home, he made a pact with himself. He would stay positive until he knew different. Suzy Greco was alive, and he was going to find her. If Neville Dakin was their man, she'd be safe while he was in custody.

The house was eerily quiet. There were no cooking smells, no television blaring away — nothing. There were several bottles of wine in the kitchen. He opened an expensive red he'd been keeping for a celebration. He'd hoped that would be when Suzy agreed to remarry him. He sat down in an armchair looking out at the garden. He rubbed his temples, trying to relax. The thing he'd forgotten just wouldn't come. He knew it was important and it had been bothering him all day. He leaned back and drank the wine. Perhaps Grace was right. If he relaxed for a while it might help.

It was dark when he woke up. The wine bottle was almost empty and he had a thick head. He'd had precious little rest, no food and there was too much on his mind. He couldn't keep this up. His thoughts kept returning to Suzy. Where was she? Was she even still alive? The thought of this made him panic again.

Panic gave him renewed energy. He went up to the bedroom. He'd go through everything, even if it took all night. Trouble was, he'd no idea what he was looking for.

Chapter 19

Day Five

Greco finished his search. He'd gone through everything, Suzy's wardrobe, her drawers, her jewellery boxes. He'd even rifled through the kitchen cupboards. But he found nothing. There were no notes, no emails on the computer. She'd either been very careful or she hadn't known her new man long.

He rustled up some toast and coffee and made a half-hearted attempt to eat. While he did, he tried Suzy's mobile again — it was still turned off. Then, as he grabbed his car keys off the dining table, he spotted it.

The flowers! He'd been wrong. They weren't from the garden at all. There was a card attached to them. He'd missed it. He'd been sitting here for most of the night and he'd not seen what was staring him in the face.

Now he had something to go on. The card read: *Suzy — can't wait until later X*. The flowers had been bought from a florist in Oldston shopping precinct. He took a sheet of newspaper and carefully wrapped them.

He checked his watch. It was almost nine. He wasn't usually this late. He'd eventually dozed off on the sofa in the early hours of the morning. The team would be getting restless and Doctor Fielding would be at the station soon. But he had to visit the florist first.

* * *

"They definitely came from us," the manager told him. "Jackie? Did you do this one?"

A young girl came in from the back of the shop and looked at the flowers. "Yes," she said.

"Who bought them?"

"We sell dozens of bouquets each day, Inspector," the manager explained. "We'll have to look through the records. If whoever bought these paid by debit or credit card then it might be easier."

"Don't you give receipts?"

She nodded.

"Then you should have a copy. There is a date on there."

"I'll have to try and work out which particular customer bought these ones. It'll take time," she said.

He looked at his watch again. "I have to get to the station." He handed her a card. "Do your checks and get back to me . . . Look, this is very important. A woman's life might depend on it. It's that serious."

He would probably have to lean on them. Whether he got anywhere or not was entirely down to their record keeping. There were no cameras in the shop, nor any on the street outside.

He made it to the station for nine thirty. The team had all arrived before him.

"Matilda alright?" he asked Grace as he passed her desk.

"She's fine — slept like a log and ate everything I put in front of her."

"Thanks, Grace. She's obviously happy with you."

"Doctor Fielding is here, sir." George said.

"Right. Speedy? You and me will do this one."

"Would you mind if I sat in?" Scarlett asked.

Greco considered this for a moment and then nodded. "Provided the doctor has no objection."

They entered the interview room with the doctor. Neville Dakin sat with his head down, staring at his hands. "I don't like it here," he told Fielding.

"They are looking after you, Neville. You are quite safe. Have you taken your pills this morning?"

"The duty doctor sorted his prescription — Amisulpride," said Greco.

"Good. He has to take them regularly."

Greco began. "This is Sergeant Quickenden and Sergeant Seddon. We had a chat yesterday. Do you remember?"

Neville shook his head. "I don't feel well," he said to Fielding.

"It's okay, Neville. Just talk to the officers. Answer their questions."

Greco produced the photos of Jessie and Jenna again. "Do you know these two girls?"

Neville pulled a face. "I did something bad. I had to. The voice made me." He pointed to Jenna. "I liked her."

"So why did you hurt her?"

"It wasn't me!" Neville was shouting now. "I had to. They don't let up. The voices said she needed sorting. I liked her but she didn't like me back. She wanted someone else. That made me mad."

"What did you do to her, Neville?" Greco said.

"I shagged her."

"Anything else?"

"I didn't cut her. It was him. I only cut a bit of her hair."

Greco looked at Speedy — the lock they'd found in Dakin's room.

"Who was with you when you cut her hair?"

"*He* was."

"Does he have a name? What do you call him?"

"I don't know. *He* never told me!" He was shouting again.

"You meet a man. You don't know him, you don't know his name, but you do whatever he asks. Is that right?"

"The voices said I had to. *He* had my pills. *He* looked after me. What was I supposed to do?"

"Do you mind if I speak to the officers about your illness, Neville?" Fielding interrupted. "It might help you if they understand."

He nodded.

"Can we go somewhere else, Inspector?"

They went into an empty room along the corridor while a uniformed officer stayed behind with Dakin.

"Neville has been ill for years," Fielding began. "But I only began treating him a few months ago. He has severe schizophrenia. He received treatment at the Meriden in Manchester, which is a specialist hospital. Schizophrenia is a psychotic illness where the patient loses touch with reality. In Neville's case it had reached the point where he was living completely in a fantasy world. He was very poorly because his condition had gone untreated for a long time. When he came to us he was a mess. Despite that, he was never violent. He lost his temper on occasions but once we'd talked it through, he was fine. On the whole, he was always relatively easy to control."

"Did he ever lash out, hurt anyone?" Scarlett asked.

"No. His temper took the form of shouting, blaming everyone for what was happening to him. He got very frustrated with his condition."

"We suspect that he was involved in the killing of those two girls. We have evidence that puts him at the scene of the murder of a young man. To me that does not sound like someone who isn't violent," Greco said.

"There has to be some mistake. Neville has never hurt anyone before. Even without medication he is placid, but the pills he takes keep him on an even keel."

"The evidence against him is building. We found his fingerprints on a poker we recovered from a crime scene. That same poker was used to kill two young women."

"There has to be some explanation." Fielding was evidently floundering.

"Yes. It's clear. He was there, and he took part. I want Dakin to talk to us. All this claptrap about voices is getting in the way. It's his excuse to do whatever he likes." Greco was angry now.

"You're wrong, Inspector. The voices are very real to Neville. He *hears* them."

"You reckon the voices have never told him to do anything violent in the past. So what's changed? Do you have any suggestions, Doctor?"

"I don't know."

"What was he like at the height of his illness?"

"Convinced he was being watched, Inspector. He was constantly trying to hide. He believed he was being listened to, that his thoughts were being monitored. That he would be found out and punished for some imagined wrong. He was timid, and felt persecuted. He most certainly was not violent."

"What if after he left hospital he stopped taking his pills?" Scarlett suggested.

She had a point, thought Greco.

"What if whoever is controlling him now has taken them from him? Substituted something else?" Scarlett said.

"It would depend what that something was," Fielding said.

"Before we go any further we will have him tested. We'll run a tox screen. Find out the truth," Greco said.

* * *

"How's it going?" Grace asked as the three returned to the main office.

"I'm not sure. We know a bit more about his medical history and we're having him tested for drugs."

Fielding came into the room. "I've taken a blood sample, Inspector. Do you want your people to test it?" He placed the phial on Greco's desk. "The tests should take no longer than twenty-four hours. Can I suggest that you allow Neville to rest until the results are in?"

"Rest? I don't think you've grasped this at all, Doctor. He is a vital piece of the puzzle — currently the only one we've got. He knows things. I need him to talk to me, not spend time flat on his back asleep." Greco was finding it difficult to control his anger. "There is a woman out there in grave danger. She may be dead. Even worse, she may be in desperate need of help!" He was shouting now. The room was silent. Apart from Grace, none of the team knew what he was talking about.

"Interrogating him again today will do no good. He'll shut us out. I know him. I know how he is when he's confused and frightened."

Greco had heard enough. He stormed out of the office. He could not sit around waiting for test results that would maybe prove Neville Dakin was high on some drug or other.

"Stephen! Wait!" Grace shouted after him. "I'm coming with you." She pulled on her jacket as they took the stairs.

"I'm going to the florist in the precinct. They should have some information for me." If they hadn't, in the mood he was in right now, he might just arrest the flaming lot of them.

"You need to calm down," she said.

"I need to find Suzy."

Chapter 20

"What was all that about?" Speedy asked the others. "Who is this other woman the boss got all riled up about?"

"There isn't one, is there?" Scarlett looked at them and then at the incident board.

"Greco has been a bit weird for the last day or two. He may not be telling us everything."

"Why wouldn't he tell us, Speedy? What's there to gain by keeping stuff to himself?" Craig asked.

"I don't know him well enough to have an opinion," Scarlett said, sitting down at her computer. "But I bet Grace knows what's going on. While we wait for that tox screen to come back, I'm going to look at the statements again and do some research."

"I'm going down to the canteen — get some coffee." Speedy was puzzled. Greco had never lost it like that before. He strode off down the corridor, only to be collared by DCI Green.

"I heard the shouting. Is everything alright?"

"Yes, sir." Speedy didn't want to elaborate. He usually did his best to avoid the DCI. He hadn't met him yet without getting a bollocking.

"Is DI Greco in the office?"

"No. He's gone to check something." Speedy tried to smile but failed.

"What's happened? Has he heard from his wife yet?"

"I don't think so, sir."

The DCI's office phone rang. Speedy took the opportunity to dart away. Greco's wife? What did that mean? As Speedy got to the canteen a terrible thought came into his mind. Was it possible that Suzy Greco was the third woman?

* * *

"Someone bought those flowers within the last couple of days. They were expensive — roses, lilies and the like. You must have some record other than a simple receipt."

"Jackie has checked them all," the manageress explained. "But it can only be one customer." She handed him a piece of paper. "It's the lilies — we should have realised. They were the expensive pink ones. We only had half a dozen in total and he bought the lot. And he paid by debit card."

Bingo — it was Neville Dakin. But that didn't make any sense. Suzy would never go for anyone like him. He was far too young. This had to be another instance of the killer laying a false trail.

"Do you remember this man?"

"Not really," Jackie replied. "We get so many folk in."

"And everyone buys expensive bouquets like this one?"

"Well, no, but we see so many faces. I'm more likely to recall the flowers rather than the person buying them."

"Do you think you'd recognise him from a photo?"

The girl shrugged and looked at her manager.

Grace nudged Greco. "You're making her nervous, sir."

"Those lilies . . ." the manageress said thoughtfully. "You were chatting, remember? About the pollen allergy."

"Ah, that man. Yes, it was him. As I was putting the blooms together, he was going on about his mother and how she couldn't be in the same room as lilies. We had a laugh about it."

"Get someone from the station to text me a photo of Dakin. Make it quick," he said to Grace.

Within a few minutes Jackie was staring at an image of Neville Dakin. "It definitely wasn't him. The man I spoke to was tall, good-looking. A bit of alright, actually. Now that I come to think about it, I quite envied his girlfriend."

"Would you recognise him, do you think?"

"I might."

"An officer will come and take a statement from you," Greco said. He and Grace left the shop.

"How dare he buy flowers for my wife," Greco muttered.

"Ex-wife, sir," Grace said.

"A mere formality."

Suddenly he stopped. Greco stood in the middle of the precinct, stock still, staring at nothing.

"The cameras! I know what's been bothering me. Mrs Hope said her husband had been at the house but we didn't pick it up. He was definitely there, so we should have seen him."

"No. Can't happen. We won't have missed him. The cameras pick up everything. We get an email when they're triggered, and anyway George monitors the images from that house constantly. She has a window open in the corner of her desktop."

Greco's stomach was churning. Their killer knew about the surveillance. Who had Greco told?

"He's done something. He's fixed the cameras so he can come and go without us knowing."

"What are you saying, sir? No one knows about the cameras except us."

"That's not strictly true. Mr and Mrs Hope know. So does the estate agent — and Laycock."

"Laycock?"

"He was on the street when they were being fitted. He guessed what was going on."

"Any one of them could have told the wrong person. We need to get down there. I'll call Speedy and get him to meet us with the keys," Grace said.

They drove in silence. If Suzy was being kept there, what were her chances? Given what had happened to the others, they weren't good.

"Speedy won't be long," Grace said. "He says not to do anything until he gets there."

Greco hardly heard her. He couldn't possibly wait. As they pulled into Percival Street he jumped out of the car and went straight to the house. "This door is heavy, made of oak. There's no way I can break in through this."

"There's no need to break in at all. The keys will be here any minute," said Grace.

Ignoring her, he checked the window. The curtains were shut tight. But the window was single glazed and large enough for him to get through. He looked around the small front garden for something he could use. He picked a large ornamental stone and hurled it at the glass.

Glass flew everywhere. Using another stone, Greco tapped out the shards left behind.

"If you must do this, use your jacket. Put it over the bottom edge before you climb inside," said Grace.

"Sir!" A voice called out behind them. "Don't! Let me go in first."

It was Speedy.

"You don't know what you're going to find in there," he said. "Better I go in first."

"He's right, sir." Grace grabbed Greco's arm. "Do you have the keys, Speedy?"

He shook his head. "Craig gave them back to the agents. Give me a few minutes. I'll get in there and see what's been going on."

They watched anxiously as Speedy eased his long legs through the smashed window.

Chapter 21

She was still, hanging limp from a beam. Her eyes were shut, her body cold. Speedy put his fingers on her wrist for a second time. He still couldn't feel a pulse. He was struggling to take in what he was looking at. Suzy Greco was trussed naked to a beam in the same manner as the other two. He didn't want to look too closely. He was terrified of finding out what had been done to her.

"Get an ambulance!" he shouted. "Tell them to make it quick."

He looked around. There was an old sofa with a knitted woollen throw over the back. He snatched it up and put it gently around Suzy Greco.

He heard banging on the door. He'd have to let them in.

"She's here, sir."

Greco rushed past him, pushing Speedy aside.

"I don't even know if she's still alive," Speedy whispered to Grace. "I can't feel a pulse and she's stone cold."

"It'll finish him if she's . . . you know . . ." Grace said.

Greco gave a strangled cry.

"She is tied up like the others. Do we take her down, or what? If she's dead, we should leave her and call the Duggan." Speedy glanced towards the room. He didn't want to go back in there.

"Speedy, you'll have to call it. This has to be your shout now."

Grace took a deep breath and went to Greco. He had taken Suzy down and was cradling her in his arms. He was muttering, his lips brushing her face.

"I can hear the ambulance siren, sir," Speedy said from the doorway.

"He's hurt her." Greco told Grace. His voice broke.

"She hasn't been burned, though. He must have intended to come back," said Grace.

"She has burns on her back. There are several small puncture wounds there."

Grace winced.

Speedy met the paramedics outside and ushered them in. The poor woman had suffered. But the injuries were not consistent with what had been done to Jessie and Jenna. They had been taken, tortured and killed in one night. This wasn't the killer's usual MO. So what had happened to make him change?

"We'll take her now," a paramedic said to Greco.

Speedy tapped him on the shoulder. "Let them help her, sir."

The medics got to work. Seconds ticked by.

"There is a faint heartbeat," one of them said finally.

Greco took a deep breath and stood back. Speedy could see that he was shaking. "You go to the hospital with her. I'll contact the Duggan." He already had his mobile in his hand. "I'll get forensics down here. We might be in with a chance. I don't think he'd finished."

"Because she isn't dead?" Greco spat out the words. "Because she wasn't hanging there with her heart burned out?"

"No . . . well . . . it's obvious. She's not been left like the others," Speedy said. "So he was coming back. It means he's not cleaned up yet."

Greco looked dazed, like he couldn't understand what Speedy was saying. He went outside and climbed into the ambulance after Suzy.

Speedy turned to face Grace. She was weeping. He grabbed hold of her arms. "I know this is bad. I know you want to help him, but you can't. The best thing we can both do for the boss now is to find this bastard, and put him away where he belongs."

Grace nodded and wiped her face.

"Good lass. It's no good getting all emotional. We need to do this right. We can't afford to miss anything."

"He did something to those cameras. We've seen none of this back at the station. So much for technology!" Grace said. She stood on a chair and looked at the camera in the sitting room. "The smart bastard had it pointing to a photo of this room. Look, Speedy. He's changed the angle and stuck the image a couple of inches away on a bracket. We were never going to see anything else."

"Very crafty."

"Damn clever if you ask me."

"What about the others?"

"The one outside failed or was deliberately tampered with. The one in the hall has been moved. It's now too high up. It could easily be avoided if you knew it was there."

"And we never noticed."

"We wouldn't, would we? All we can see is the top of the door and part of the hallway."

Grace snapped on a pair of nitrile gloves and gently removed the photo. She touched only the corner to preserve any prints or evidence on it.

"You knew, didn't you? About his wife?" Speedy said.

"Ex-wife. And yes, he told me."

"How long has she been missing?"

"The morning after you dealt with that body in the park. She was having an affair. He saw her with the bloke that afternoon. They were kissing by the boating pool."

"That's why he went all weird on me."

"He got some CCTV from the college. It showed her getting into the Focus. That was when he knew."

"We've still got Dakin in custody," Speedy said. Could that be the reason the killer hadn't come back?

"Dakin didn't do this. Suzy Greco would never go for a man like that. He's too young and too stupid. Dakin was being manipulated. We just need to find out who was pulling the strings."

* * *

"Speedy!" Craig greeted him as he and Grace walked into the main office. "Doctor Atkins from the Duggan has been on. She wanted Greco but you'll have to do."

"I'll ring her back. Anything exciting?"

"She didn't say. Where is Greco anyway?"

"He's gone to the hospital with Suzy, his ex. We found her at that house on Percival Street."

"What was she doing there? Is she okay?" Scarlett asked.

"No, I don't think she is," Grace replied, biting her lip. "She'd been taken by this monster we're looking for. It was really awful. She was trussed to a beam like the others and he'd started to hurt her. Speedy said she was cold. I thought she'd gone, but the medics found a pulse and whisked her off."

"We'll just have to get on without him. That means all of us, Grace. The best way to deal with this is to find the bastard," Speedy said. He rang Roxy Atkins. He'd been wanting to ask her out since their first meeting, but now obviously wasn't the time.

"Your prisoner," she began. "We got the blood sample but given it's drugs we're testing for, I came over, took another sample and ran a saliva test too — the results

181

are in quicker. The drug your suspect's been taking is crystal meth, probably in tablet form. There was little evidence in his blood of the anti-psychotic drug he should have been taking, so the meth was most likely substituted for his usual pills."

"Thanks, Roxy."

"Crystal meth," he told the others. "We need to talk to that doctor from Springbank again."

Ignoring Speedy, Grace said, "Someone set that room up. And that someone knew about the cameras. They sabotaged them. Greco told me that, apart from us, the Hopes and the estate agent, only one other person knew about them — Oliver Laycock from the *Herald*."

"You think it's him?" Craig asked doubtfully.

"I don't know. But perhaps we should find out what he was doing on the nights the girls were killed, and if he was the one seeing Suzy. We might not like him, but he is a good-looking guy and the age is right."

"We'll bring him in," Speedy said. "Craig, you can come with me. We'll try the *Herald's* offices first. Grace, would you and Scarlett speak to the doctor? Find out how crystal meth would affect someone like Dakin."

"I'll have to have a cup of tea first," Grace told Scarlett. "Seeing her like that — it really shook me up."

* * *

"You are having a laugh," Laycock bellowed at the two detectives. "If you want to speak to me it'll have to be here. I'm a busy man. I don't have time to waste in your poxy station."

"You don't have much choice, Mr Laycock. If you don't come willingly, I'll arrest you," said Speedy.

"This is a load of rubbish. I'm a reporter, not a criminal — despite the rumours. I know your boss doesn't like me. If this turns out to be a waste of time, I'll make mincemeat of the lot of you. You're already a hot topic in my column."

They drove in silence back to the station. The reporter was left to wait in an interview room.

"Do we have any background on him?" Speedy asked.

George tapped away on her computer. "There's very little. He's married — no children. And he's a member of Leesworth golf club."

"C'mon, Craig, let's get this done with." They went into the interview room.

"Right, Laycock. I want you to get your thinking cap on. I want a full rundown of your whereabouts from last weekend onwards."

"That's a lot of time, Sergeant." Laycock looked at his mobile. "Last weekend, nothing. Worked every day until about six. I had a drink and a meal with your boss in the Crown a couple of nights ago." He smiled smugly at them. "Apart from that — more nothing."

"Can anyone vouch for all this *nothing* you do?"

"Why? Is it important? What do you think I've done?"

"Do you know either of these young women?" Speedy put the photos of Jessie and Jenna in front of him.

"Yes, I know her." He pointed to the one of Jessie. "She used to work in the Crown until she was murdered." He stared at the detectives, his eyes jumping from one to the other. "You think I know something?"

"Do you?"

"No. Last time I looked, that was your job."

"You still haven't told us what you were doing, Mr Laycock," Craig said.

"I'd prefer not to."

"That could give you a problem." Speedy looked at Craig and they both nodded.

"No. It gives you a problem. I haven't done anything. You are wasting your time. Time that would be better spent catching the real murderer."

"Make yourself comfortable. Until I get a proper answer, you'll be staying here."

Speedy got to his feet and gathered up the papers from the desk.

"Okay. I was at home. When I'm not working, I'm always at home."

Speedy sat down again. "Go on. Tell us more."

Laycock was silent. Speedy's fingers drummed on the desktop.

"My wife has MS. After six I'm her main carer. Same at weekends. She's looked after during the day while I'm at work, but the rest is down to me."

"And someone will vouch for that?"

"The nurses who attend, the carers — an entire army of people, Sergeant," he said. He sounded resigned.

"I'll check it out."

"You'll need this." He wrote down a phone number on Speedy's notepad. "That's our GP. Ring him. I'll give him the nod and he'll give you any further information you need."

* * *

"If you don't mind me saying, you are getting too involved with the DI."

"I do mind, Scarlett. It's none of your business. We're friends — well, sort of friends. He talks to me. We have stuff in common. It's nothing else, despite what folk might think."

"The truth is, you've got the hots for him but he's not interested. Admit it — it's not a sin, you know."

Grace didn't reply. Scarlett Seddon was irritating her. Goodness knows what she said to the others when she was out. She might be bright but she needed to tone it down or she'd end up antagonising everyone.

"Springbank House." Grace nodded at the imposing Victorian building. "I'll park outside."

Edna Rowcroft let them in. Her only comment was, "I hope you're looking after Neville."

184

"Could we have a word with Doctor Fielding?" Scarlett asked.

They followed her down the corridor and into a sitting room. She pointed to a sofa and left.

"She doesn't approve of what we've done." Scarlett nudged Grace. "Does my head in. Do-gooders and their misguided notions."

"Despite what they might think we had no choice but to arrest him, did we? Dakin took part in those murders. The evidence is stacking up. What we have to determine now is whether he's mad or bad," said Grace.

"And get him to tell us who he was with," Scarlett said. "All this nonsense about not knowing his name. It's a joke."

Fielding came into the room.

"Do you have any news?" he said.

"We know that Dakin wasn't taking his usual medication. What we don't know is how long for. Instead, he'd been taking crystal meth — in tablet form. What we need to know is how a drug like that would affect someone like Neville."

Grace had put it as simply as she could. She hoped the doctor's explanation would be equally clear.

"Crystal meth in tablet form . . ." he repeated thoughtfully. "That wouldn't do Neville any good at all. It would amplify the hallucinations. It would make the voices he hears appear more real. He would be living entirely in a world of his imagination."

"Or someone else's," Scarlett said. "Is that possible? Would he do as he was told — even if it was something really bad?"

Fielding's eyebrows rose.

"It is possible. If the dosage was large enough and Neville felt afraid. In any event he'd certainly have erratic mood swings. Yes — he could become violent."

"So he could be controlled? Someone else could dictate his actions?" Grace asked.

"Yes, I suppose they could. In Neville's head this someone else you speak of would be the voice made real. Under the drug's influence he would no longer understand the difference between good and bad. He would be susceptible to any orders he was given — wise or not."

"Currently we are presuming that there was someone influencing him. Do you have any idea who that might be?" Scarlett asked.

"He stayed here as an in-patient before he went to live alone."

"Did he have visitors?" Grace added.

"I don't recall any. Even when he was doing well, Neville didn't trust people. And generally people didn't like Neville very much."

"Any phone calls, enquiries about his wellbeing?" Grace said.

Fielding shook his head.

"So he had no contact at all with the outside world?"

"That's right. He spoke to people here, other patients. The carers quite liked him — Edna particularly."

"Do you keep a log of visitors and the phone calls made to patients?" Grace asked.

"Visitors, yes — but as I said before, Neville didn't have any."

"Thank you, Doctor. We will have to interview Neville again. Given what we know about the drugs he took it would be helpful if you were his appropriate adult this time," Grace said.

Fielding nodded. "I'll be pleased to help."

Chapter 22

"What have we got?" Speedy asked the team.

"The crystal meth would have made Dakin even worse. To para-phrase Fielding, he'd be a pushover. He'd do anything he was told."

"Laycock is in the clear," Speedy said.

"To be honest, I never really thought it was him," Grace said.

"So who are we looking for? We have nothing. No visual evidence, no DNA. This man isn't a phantom. He's flesh and blood, and he'll have made mistakes." Speedy was at the end of his tether.

"He only needs to make one," Grace said. "We just have to find it."

"Has anyone heard from the hospital?" Scarlett asked. "The DI's wife is evidence, don't forget."

"She's a lot more than that and she's his ex-wife," Grace said. "I'm reluctant to ring and ask. I can't face hearing the answer."

"Has Greco not rung in?"

"No, Craig. He has better things to think about."

"What about the kid? Do you need to go?" Speedy asked.

"I've organised my mum to help, so it's fine."

"I think I might have found something." George looked up from her computer.

"Go on," Speedy said.

"Naturally I searched the database for murders with a similar MO. I concentrated on the poker and the burning — it's pretty unique. But I got nothing. Now I've widened the criteria. During the last five years there have been three other instances where a number of young women were murdered. A single male perpetrator was caught in each case. In one of those instances, it was presumed that another had got away, but there was no evidence. There were eight girls murdered in total. In all cases, the one that was apprehended had been receiving treatment for a psychiatric illness. When tested, the one who was caught was found to have been taking crystal meth instead of their usual medication. They were all deemed unfit to plead and sent to secure institutions. Like I said, in only one of those cases did the investigating officers think it likely that there was someone else — the brains if you like. And they thought he was the one that had done the planning."

"And he was never caught. Where were these?" Grace asked.

"Three women on the South Coast, two in Nottingham and another three in Carlisle. But here is the clincher." She paused, checking her data again. "In each run of killings, the final woman taken was always someone close to the SIO. The wife of a DCI, the daughter of another and in Carlisle, the wife of a DI."

"That is some coincidence!" Speedy exclaimed.

"Well, it's not, is it? It has to be him — our killer. He's taken Suzy so this run is finished. How did he kill the other women, George?" Grace said.

"They were all restrained, the first three to chairs. They had their throats cut. The next two were poisoned and the last three had arteries opened and bled to death."

Speedy winced. "This is some sick bastard. Anything else?"

"He tortured and sexually assaulted them all before killing them. But it's interesting about the last victim," George said.

"The one close to the senior investigating officer?"

"Yes, Grace. In all cases, the mode of killing was an overdose of morphine administered by injection."

"Are there any details on there that we can use?"

"No — and believe me, I've looked very carefully. He's clever and he's clean. There were never any fingerprints, DNA or anything else left behind."

"So this person is still a phantom?" Speedy shook his head. This just got worse.

"And the killings? They just stopped?" Grace looked at George's screen.

"Looking at the different locations, it appears he moved on. He must have that kind of job," George said.

"So now he'll be planning to move again. Someone should tell Greco. The bit about the morphine is important."

"I'll ring the hospital," Scarlett said. "I'm less involved than the rest of you."

The office phone rang. The team looked at one another. No one wanted to hear the bad news. Finally Grace picked it up.

"Is there any news on Suzy?"

"Who is this?" Grace asked.

"Jill Brayshaw from Oldston College. I work with Suzy. Only, Stephen was in here looking for her. I didn't realise at the time but she has left her mobile on charge in the staffroom. If she's still missing there might be something on it that will help."

"Don't touch it. Leave it plugged in and I'll come and collect it. Thank you for letting us know."

Grace turned to the others. "Suzy left her mobile at college. Given that she was seeing this maniac, what's the betting they rang each other or texted."

"Are you alright to go get it?"

"Yes, Speedy, and I won't be long."

As Grace left the office, the phone rang again. This time it was Natasha Barrington.

"Sergeant Quickenden," she began. "I need you to come to the Duggan as soon as you can. We have a situation and a member of your team should be present."

"Want to tell me more?"

"Not over the phone. It's delicate and . . . rather upsetting. Just get over here."

"Okay. I'll leave right away."

"I'll print all this out and give you copies," George told the team.

Speedy didn't tell them about the phone call. He was puzzled and worried. He had an awful feeling that this wasn't going to be good.

* * *

"It's been plugged in all this time and I never even noticed," Jill Brayshaw explained.

"Did you know Suzy was seeing someone else?"

"I had my suspicions. The usual stuff — hair, make-up, buying new clothes. And she was never off that thing." She nodded at the mobile.

"Did you meet him?"

Jill shook her head. "Suzy never actually said anything. There was plenty of teasing, but she never came clean."

"Did you ever see him from the window or when he came to pick her up?"

"No. I never saw them together. I don't think it'd been going on for very long. Is she okay? We haven't heard anything since she disappeared."

She didn't know. "Suzy was kidnapped," Grace said gently. "She's been hurt and has been taken to hospital. Stephen is with her."

"I'd no idea." Jill Brayshaw sat down. "Did he have anything to do with it? The man she was seeing?"

Grace nodded. She unplugged the phone and turned it on. "Suzy's kidnap is part of a much larger enquiry," she explained.

It was an iPhone. She needed the pin number.

"I don't suppose you know the pin for this?" Grace said. Jill Brayshaw shook her head.

Grace could give it to the techies to crack, but that would take time. She had one of these herself. Her pin was Holly's date of birth. It was worth a try. "Do you know when Matilda's birthday is?"

"April, I think. The second — same as my gran's."

Grace tapped in the four digits. It was wrong. The pin wasn't based on the day, month and year — perhaps the year alone? Aware that she only had so many goes to get this right, she tried again. It worked!

"You've done it?" Jill looked impressed.

"Us mothers, we're all the same," Grace smiled. "She used Matilda's birth year. I do something similar."

Grace scanned down the list of calls. There were dozens. Grace recognised Greco's number. Next she studied the texts. There were several — all signed 'X.' That had to be him.

"Thanks. I'll tell Stephen to let you know how she's doing," Grace said.

Back in her car, Grace rang the station. "George, can you find out who owns a particular mobile for me?" She gave her the number.

"You do realise it's probably a pay-as-you-go?"

"It's worth checking anyway. Is Speedy there?"

"No, he's gone out. He didn't say where or why."

"Have we heard from the boss?"

"No. And no one has rung him either."

"Okay. Ring me back when you get the info on that number."

Grace knew that Greco had no one in Oldston other than Suzy and his daughter. Her parents lived in Norfolk, so even if he'd told them, they wouldn't be here yet. He'd be at the hospital all alone. She didn't want to intrude but she decided to go and find out for herself how Suzy was.

Parking at Oldston General was always a problem, but Grace knew a back street only a few yards from a side entrance. She went straight to A&E.

"You'll have to speak to a doctor," the receptionist said to Grace.

"Is she in one of the cubicles?"

The woman shook her head.

Perhaps she'd been transferred to another department — intensive care or somewhere else. She might even be on the operating table. But where was Greco?

Chapter 23

Grace decided to wait. She took a seat in A&E and had another look at the phone. Most of the texts the killer had sent to Suzy gave very little away. There were load of flirty messages and some making plans to meet. Then she found one that was interesting. In this one he was having a right moan. Apparently he'd been asked to work late and wasn't going to be able to see her. He wrote that there had been a break-in and his team were needed. He also said he hated having to work in a coverall. He wrote that one day he'd get a job in the city and go to work in a proper suit instead.

Did that mean he was a cop, or even a CSI? The wording of the text gave that impression.

Grace's phone rang. It was Greco.

"Stephen! How are you? How's Suzy?" Grace got to her feet and began pacing up and down. "I'm sorry, I don't want to intrude but I knew you'd be on your own. I'm at the hospital. I can meet you if you tell me what ward you're on."

"It's good of you, but I'm not there."

"Where are you?"

"At the Duggan. Have you got anything else?"

"I might have. It's something I found literally just this minute. Why have you gone to the Duggan? I don't understand. Have they found something?"

"I've got to go. Keep me informed," he said. He hadn't answered her question.

"Before you go, I have to tell you something. It's likely that Suzy was given an overdose of morphine. Tell the doctors treating her. It's important."

He rang off.

Grace's mobile rang again, earning her a stern look from one of the nurses.

"George, what have you got?"

"It's a pay-as-you-go. Not registered to anyone and used to call only one number."

Grace knew which number — Suzy's. "You were right – pity. Thanks, George. I'll be back shortly."

"You haven't told me how she is," George said.

"Because I can't," Grace's voice wavered. "No one will tell me and Greco isn't here. Is Speedy back yet?"

"No."

"Look, I'm off to the Duggan. I won't be long. Tell Speedy when he comes back."

Greco shouldn't be there. He should be with his wife. Something was wrong. Why would no one tell her anything? Why would he go to the Duggan? What had he found out? Her stomach churned. Something told her this was going to be a bumpy ride.

* * *

"You can't go in there," Natasha Barrington told Greco. "You know that. You shouldn't even be here," she said kindly. "Look — I'll get you a cup of tea. Go and sit down in my office until it's over, then I'll come and talk to you."

"I want to know everything. Don't hold back because it's Suzy."

"We'll see," she replied.

194

"Will anyone from the team attend?"

"Sergeant Quickenden is here. He's speaking to Roxy at present. I asked him to come so he could be with you. Shall I send him in?"

"Okay," Greco agreed. "But I don't want him in there when . . ."

"I understand. It'll just be me and my staff."

He didn't want anyone seeing what was about to happen to Suzy. How could he work with Speedy again knowing he had been present at her post-mortem? It was a private, intimate thing. She would be lying there exposed and vulnerable. Her body would be opened up, examined and photographed. Greco started to weep. He was lost, stumbling through a nightmare.

"Doctor Barrington said you were here."

It was Speedy, holding two mugs of tea.

"She told me. I'm sorry, sir. I don't know what to say. I hoped we'd found her in time. We did everything we could — got her to the hospital fast. It's all so awful. Should you be here?"

"I don't know where I should be. I can't believe what's happened. I can't believe she's gone."

"We will get him. He'll have slipped up somewhere. He's done it before, sir." Speedy told him about George's research.

"I'm not sure that helps. We still don't know who he is."

"George is trawling through the other case notes. There might be something."

"Has Dakin said anything?"

"Not when I left. He's incapable of saying anything coherent."

"When today is over, you'll have to take this on. Look at the report and deal with any issues. I won't be allowed to get involved. I know I have no right to ask, but I want you to keep me in the loop. You have to get this bastard, Speedy. I'm relying on you."

* * *

Grace pulled into the Duggan car park. Speedy's car was here. Perhaps he'd come to pick up Greco. Whatever the reason, she had other things to think about. She'd checked the date on the text. It was two weeks ago. She rang George.

"A break-in. I'm presuming it was local. I need to know who attended. In fact, anything you can find. And I need it quick."

He'd mentioned a coverall and he'd attended that incident — if it not something he'd invented. She waited in her car. She didn't want to go inside until she had something. Speedy and Greco were both in there and she wanted something concrete to tell them. Suzy's phone was a start, but on its own it wasn't enough. Grace checked all the images while she waited, but there was nothing helpful. There were plenty of Matilda and some of the house but none of her new boyfriend.

Within five minutes George got back to her.

"Ainsworth Engineering. You were right, it was a robbery. One of the office staff working late was coshed over the head so they had CSI round and they gave it the works."

"From the Duggan?"

"Yes."

"Thanks, George. I'll be back later."

Grace went straight to Roxy Atkins's office.

"They are in with Tasha at the moment," Roxy said.

"Greco and Speedy. It's okay. I need a word with you first."

"First, I must tell you what I've got." She moved over to her computer. "That photo you gave me — the image of the sitting room at Percival Street."

Grace nodded.

"There were no fingerprints, but we did find something else — pollen. Pollen from a pink lily."

"The killer gave Suzy a bouquet. Greco was going on about it. I was with him when he went to the florists to find out who'd sent it."

"And did he? Find out?"

"It was bought and paid for in the name of Neville Dakin — so no, we didn't, not really."

"It's something to think about anyway. What did you want a word about?"

"A fortnight ago a team from here attended a break-in." Grace showed her the address in her notepad. "I'd like to know who was on the forensic team that went out on that night."

"Is it important?"

"Yes. I think one of them is our killer."

Roxy Atkins looked at her, open-mouthed. "Surely not. You must have that wrong. Our people are all thoroughly checked."

"I'm looking for someone who hasn't been here long. If he hasn't spun you a pack of lies, he's worked in Carlisle, the South Coast and Nottingham. Does that ring any bells?"

"The latest additions to the team here are me and Mark Brough. I came here from Liverpool, where I'd worked for the last five years. Mark came to us highly qualified and with excellent references, as I recall. I'll check his file. But I think you must have this wrong. Mark is charming. Your colleague certainly thinks so. They are on the verge of arranging a date, so he told me." She winked.

Trust Scarlett! Grace waited while Roxy checked his work file on the computer.

"Mark was on the Ainsworth Engineering job that night," she confirmed. Her face was serious. "And you're right. He's worked in all the places you mentioned. Are you sure you've not made a mistake?"

Grace felt sick. "There is no mistake, Roxy. I have Suzy's phone. He texted her. He used that job as the reason why they couldn't meet that day. Where is he now?"

"With the team doing the PM."

"I need to see him."

"You can't go in there," Roxy said. "It's Suzy Greco's PM they are doing."

Grace felt sick. "Suzy . . . she didn't make it. I didn't know. No one at the hospital said anything to me. Greco will be in bits." She looked at Roxy. "He's not actually in there? Mark Brough?"

"Yes, he is."

"I think I'm going to be sick." She felt the room swirl. "I want to go in. Let me onto the viewing platform."

"Are you okay? You've gone grey."

"Are you surprised? That man is some piece of work. He must truly believe he's untouchable." Grace was furious. She had all the pieces now to pin this where it belonged. And that was what she was going to do. The pollen came from the flowers he had given Suzy. He had the right background. What she had to do now was bring it all together by proving that he'd made those phone calls and written those texts to Suzy.

Roxy led the way and unlocked the door that led into the morgue. "Tasha said I wasn't to let any of your team in here. Greco specifically asked."

"If I'm right, he won't mind, believe me."

"What are you going to do?"

"Surprise him," Grace said. "He's caused enough pain. Now it ends. Ring the station for me. Get the troops here."

Her legs felt wobbly. Grace could see Suzy's body, pale and lifeless on the slab. She didn't want to look and she didn't want to listen to the clatter of stainless steel or the slosh of internal organs.

Natasha Barrington was logging the injuries one by one. No one noticed Grace come in. They were all intent on the job. Mark Brough was taking the samples as

Natasha handed them to him, and the camera flashed at regular intervals.

Grace took her own phone from her pocket and rang Speedy. "Don't talk. Just listen," she whispered. "Go and stand outside the morgue Doctor Barrington's working in and stop anyone who comes out. No exceptions. Stop them dead. Do you understand?"

Now she took Suzy Greco's phone from her bag. It was a risk. He might not even have his mobile on him. But it was worth a shot. Her finger hovered over the number. If she'd got it wrong, she was in trouble. More than that, Greco would never forgive her. Her hand was shaking. This was risky. But George had given her the details and Roxy had confirmed them. What more did she need? Grace knew she was in shock. She had to sharpen up.

Grace pressed the number. There was a second or two of quiet and then the sharp trill of a mobile phone broke the silence in the morgue. Grace smiled with relief. He must have the mobile in his pocket. Brough was their man. It was Mark Brough who had killed the girls and Suzy Greco. She'd got him.

"Phones are not allowed in here," Natasha Barrington barked at her assistant.

"My fault, I'm afraid!" Grace called out. "Mark Brough, you are under arrest for—"

He turned round. His look made the words catch in her throat. Seconds ticked by. Everyone had frozen in place like a scene from a play. Suddenly Mark Brough darted for the exit.

* * *

"What are you running from?" Speedy grabbed Brough's arm as he crashed through the door.

"Get off! That bitch has flipped. She's made a huge mistake. This has nothing to do with me."

"Speedy!" Grace called. "It's him! He's our killer."

Speedy had no idea where this came from, but Grace was rarely wrong.

"You're sure?"

"Yes! Suzy's phone — he called her, texted, they were seeing one another."

Speedy gave her a doubtful look. "Is that it?" His grip on Brough's arm loosened.

"No. There's other stuff." She nodded at the uniformed officers coming down the corridor. "Take him to the station and make sure he doesn't go anywhere," Grace instructed them.

"Where's Greco?"

"In Doctor Barrington's office. I said I was going for more coffee. He knows nothing of your call — or this."

"I'll speak to him."

"You'd better have this right." Speedy followed after her. "There is nothing in the way of forensics."

"Oh, there is." She turned and smiled. "They've got pollen off that photo we found. And he's done this before. Other forces will have stuff. now we have a name, we'll nail him, Speedy. He won't walk this time."

Chapter 24

Day Six

Speedy and Grace sat down facing Brough. He was whispering to his solicitor.

"I suggest you save us all a lot of trouble and let me out of here now," he said with a smile.

So charming. He was smooth-talking and confident. He'd been kept in the cells overnight and had been cool and calm throughout. He'd engaged one of the officers in conversation. The officer said Brough had even cracked a joke or two. It made Grace feel sick.

Brough sat back in the chair, relaxed, sipping on the coffee he'd been given.

"I'm afraid we can't do that, Mr Brough," Grace replied just as smoothly. "You have been charged with several very serious offences."

"As I have tried to explain, you've got it completely wrong. And I'm not just saying that. I mean it. I have experience in this business, don't forget. I know you have nothing. There was nothing left behind. I read the notes."

"When you did that, Mr Brough, the notes were incomplete. The case against you was made in the final hours. During that time we found damning evidence against you."

His laugh became a cough and he sipped more coffee. "Okay, so I was having a fling with Suzy Greco. I texted her, rang her and saw her a few times." He leaned forward. "But I did not kill her."

"Yes, you did, and not only her." Grace put the photos of Jessie and Jenna on the desk. "You brutally murdered these two young women."

"You are insane! Like I said before, where is the evidence?"

"The phone, and your background. Women have been killed in three locations you've worked in."

"Not enough. That is circumstantial — the CPS will throw it out."

"We are in contact with the other forces," Speedy added. "They are looking at the evidence again, the case notes. There will be something."

"And of course there is the flower pollen." Grace said.

There was a silence. Mark Brough stared at Grace's impassive face.

"What did you say?"

"The pollen. It came from the pink lilies you bought for Suzy. The florist confirmed it. She admired your taste. They were expensive, but you know that. After all, you paid for them. But perhaps you don't know how rare they are at this time of year. The florist in Oldston only had ten and you bought the lot. You bought them with a debit card in the name of Neville Dakin. At this time of year folk tend to buy daffodils, tulips. They're cheaper, you see. So the assistant remembers — and she remembers *you*, Mr Brough."

"The girl there can identify you," Speedy added. "Then of course there is Neville Dakin. He will identify you too. Not so easy to wriggle out of now, is it?"

"Dakin's a halfwit!" Brough exclaimed. "I can't believe this. You're joking, aren't you? The reality is you've got nothing! I don't make those kinds of mistakes."

"Yes, you do, Mr Brough. Even you can cock it up occasionally." Speedy said.

It was in his eyes — the disbelief that he, of all people, could make such a fundamental error.

"You're joking?" he said.

Grace hunched her shoulders. "Are we, Mark? We've got you thinking though, haven't we?" She leaned forward. "You remember those flowers and you remember the pollen too. I can see it in your face. You've messed up — time to admit what you've done."

A muscle in Brough's face began to twitch, for the first time he looked frightened. The mask had slipped. They had him.

"Do you want to tell us why now, Mark?" Speedy asked.

Brough gave him a murderous look. "Police — that's why. A waste of space the bloody lot of you."

"That's an opinion, it's not a reason to kill innocent young women or target families of those in the force."

"I have my reasons," he scowled back. "The police ruined my life. I had a wife of my own once. She left me for some smart-arsed copper on his way up. Then they tried to get me sacked, the pair of them." He paused, his face had paled at the recollection.

"Go on, Mark, finish your story," Speedy prompted.

"He said I'd removed evidence from the site of murder case his team was investigating. I hadn't, no way. I was eventually exonerated. He was hauled over the coals by his superintendent and took it out on my wife. I had tried to warn her but she wouldn't listen. He was a bully, just like the rest of you."

"How, Mark? What happened to her?"

He looked at Speedy with hate in his eyes. "She was only young. He killed her. He didn't care, thought he could get away with it, and was right. Beat her to death, made it look like a violent break-in. He knew how to make it look kosher," he smiled. "You people protecting the public, eh?"

"And that's why you do this?" Grace asked.

"Why not? It gave me a sense of purpose. After the first two, I began to enjoy it. The force ruined my life. They should be made to pay. As for those girls — they were a bonus. They were like my wife, slappers and out for what they could get. They're all the bloody same."

Grace felt sick at his twisted, stupid, hateful logic.

Epilogue

"Should you be here, sir?" Craig said.

Greco sat down at his desk. "Probably not."

"This is not a good idea. You must have stuff to do at home." Grace looked up from a pile of paperwork.

"Suzy's parents are dealing with the funeral. It's not for another week. They want to sort her house too." He gave a half-hearted smile. "I feel like a spare part around them. They are taking care of Matilda. They're taking care of everything."

"They're only trying to protect you," Grace said.

"No. They blame me. They never did like the idea of Suzy being together with a copper. Her dad always said it would get her into bother one day."

"Well, the good news is we got him," Grace said. "He told us everything. In the end we couldn't shut him up. The maniac was proud of what he'd done, of how he'd just walked away so many times."

"He gave us an explanation of sorts in the end," Speedy added. "The man was driven by his demons. Makes no sense to right-minded folk, but then the likes of Mark Brough are psychopaths, so the rules go out the window."

Demons, Greco knew all about them. What had happened to Suzy would haunt him for the rest of his life. He couldn't sleep without seeing the image of her hanging there in that room. He wanted to weep each time he glimpsed a photo of her, or Matilda mentioned her name. He had no idea how he was going to get over any of this.

"You all did a great job. Grace, George, the four of you — and Scarlett. Where is she, by the way?" He sounded almost normal. But then they couldn't see the turmoil in his head.

"She's gone back to Daneside," Grace said and smiled.

"You pieced this together with no help from me. After Suzy — I just fell apart." He knew that sounded glib but he didn't want to break down in front of his colleagues, understanding as they were.

"She was your wife, you had every right to," said Grace.

"Ex-wife. Like you kept reminding me — and she was seeing another man."

"Nevertheless, you were close and she was Matilda's mother. You really should go home. You don't look yourself at all."

Greco knew he looked a mess. He'd slept in his clothes and he hadn't shaved. He hardly recognised himself when he looked in the mirror. "I don't do time off very well. Matilda is staying with her grandparents at Suzy's house, so I'm back in the flat. I'll go mad sitting on my own with nothing to do."

"I'm not tiptoeing around this," Grace said firmly. "You look like crap. The DCI said you had to take time off. So you should take it. And think of Matilda. She's just lost her mum. You don't want her worrying about her dad too. If you don't see her, she'll fret."

"I'm thinking of moving on, actually." He put his head in his hands.

They stared at him in disbelief. Then they all spoke at once, all protesting.

"Why do that? You're settled here now," Grace said.

"I came to Oldston because Matilda was here with Suzy. The chances are that now she'll go back to Norfolk with her grandparents."

"Speak to her. Ask the child what she wants to do. Being a single parent isn't easy, but you will get by. I do. And I'll lay odds she'll want to stay with you."

Greco shrugged. He wasn't sure that was even what he wanted. Work was so demanding that he'd rarely see the child. She'd grow up with no mother and a part-time father. Could he do that to her?

"Stephen, I saw you pass my office door. Can I have a word, please?" DCI Green asked, popping his head round the corner.

Now he'd get it from the boss too. "I'm climbing the walls at home," he said, as they walked down the corridor.

"But home is where you belong. Those aren't just words, Stephen. I'm probably the only person here who appreciates something of what you're going through. I lost my first wife twenty years ago — traffic accident on the M62. It was a dreadful time. I was ready to give up the lot. She left me with the twins — five years old, they were."

This was a revelation. Greco had had no idea.

"You managed?"

"Yes, I did. But don't be misled. It was tough. After a while things settle but you're the one left with the reality. This is no time to be putting on a brave face. I took the time off, and so should you. The job will still be here. You will have to make changes, compromise. But what matters is how you move forward with your daughter. The pair of you have to build a different life."

"She has her grandparents."

"She needs you. When Angie died, I almost made the same mistake. Her parents were only too willing to take the girls. We were in the middle of a case and I got my priorities wrong. In the end, I realised what was important and I let it go. The team coped without me, as yours did. If you don't take the time to grieve, within weeks you'll be a mess. I didn't come back to work until I could see things more clearly. I made use of the system and the kindness of friends and family."

Greco hadn't a clue about any of this. But then why should he? He was still getting to know Colin Green.

They reached the DCI's office and he gestured for Greco to sit down.

"You should know that what you and your team did hasn't gone unnoticed. Brough was a serial killer no one was even aware of. The forces in the locations he'd operated in suspected there was someone else, but they had no proof. He could have kept killing for a long time."

"And getting away with it," Greco said with disgust. "He set Dakin up good and proper. Gave him a car and a debit card, and purchases were all made in that young man's name."

"The new task force — the major incident team — has finally got the go-ahead. It will be put together within the next couple of months. You have been put forward as the DCI who should lead it."

Greco was stunned. "I couldn't possibly take it on. My head's all over the place. They'll have to look for someone else."

"I know now is not a good time. I've told them upstairs and no one is pushing you. You've been through a nightmare. I can't begin to imagine the horror you must have felt in that room. There is counselling available, you know. You should consider it."

Greco dipped his eyes. He didn't want sympathy, it made him weep, and he didn't want counselling. He'd had enough of that with his OCD.

"I wouldn't have broached the new job at all, but the super insisted that I should. He sees it as a great opportunity. At any other time in your life I would agree with him. But I have stressed that you must not be hurried into this."

"So I can think about it?"

"Take as much time as you need," Green said kindly.

"It's a far bigger job," Greco shook his head. The doubts were already there. "The sacrifice might be too much," he looked at Green. "I'm thinking of Matilda. I'd end up seeing even less of her."

"A father drowning under the weight of tragedy is no good for her either. I know it's small consolation but ultimately it might be good for both of you. You are ambitious, Stephen, I know that."

"My team here?"

"You don't have to think about the details now. But you will have a say in the make-up of the new team. Some of the officers here might be happy to transfer with you."

"Okay, I'll give it some thought."

"That's all I ask, Stephen. But wait a few weeks until this is less raw. The decision on how to move forward is yours alone. Personally, I wouldn't want the force to lose you. But, given what's happened I understand the difficulties you face."

Greco walked back to the main office in a daze. Did he want this? What should he tell his colleagues? More to the point, who would he want to take with him?

"Give you a hard time, sir?"

"No, Speedy. Quite the reverse. I think he might have just thrown me a lifeline."

THE END

Thank you for reading this book. If you enjoyed it please leave feedback on Amazon, and if there is anything we missed or you have a question about then please get in touch. The author and publishing team appreciate your feedback and time reading this book.

Our email is jasper@joffebooks.com

www.joffebooks.com